By Special Delivery

Richard Stoll

© Richard Stoll 2018

All rights reserved

ISBN: 978 - 0 - 244 - 44305 - 4

Distributed by Lulu Press Inc.
(www.lulu.com)

Preface

After working hard as bricklayer's labourer for several months, Jack is attracted by a mysterious advertisement for a two very fit young people to undertake an unspecified task involving arduous hiking in the mountains. Following a successful interview, he finds himself teamed up with Lucy, an ultra-fit exercise fanatic who seems to think that she could quite easily do the job on her own.

However, everything is not as it seems. Not only is the task assigned to them quite extraordinary and possibly dangerous, but even self-assured Lucy slowly comes realize that she needs Jack's support more than she thought possible, especially when they get a nasty surprise and are saved by what can only be described as divine intervention.

Cover picture:

The Wetterhorn near Grindelwald, Switzerland

Chapter 1: Called to Carlisle

A newspaper, folded back at an inside page, lay discarded on a chair in Jack's favourite café. He was just about to turn to the front page to read the headlines while he sipped his coffee when his eyes alighted on a small advertisement.

"Wanted for an unusual and challenging job: two very fit young people between the ages of 19 and 24 to undertake a task lasting approximately five weeks. A period of preparation will take place prior to travelling to central Europe where arduous hiking over mountainous terrain will be required. Possession of a valid passport is essential. Applications in writing with full CVs should be sent to PO Box No. 27, Carlisle before 25th April. Interviews will be conducted in Carlisle on 6th May."

Recently made redundant from a building company in Leeds, Jack's interest was immediately aroused. He had been working as a bricklayer's labourer for almost seven months while he searched for a job after graduating in Biomaterials Science and Engineering at Sheffield University. Although only short-term, the advertisement sounded intriguing.

As a mere labourer, he had done very little bricklaying but an enormous amount of lugging heavy loads of bricks and mortar from one place to another. This had had the advantage of hardening his already strong frame; whereas, at the start, he had been completely shattered by the end of the day, now he could survive a full shift without difficulty.

For the last few months, he had even enjoyed helping out twice a week at a boy's fitness club near his flat in one of the poorer city suburbs. It was a voluntary job he enjoyed; not just for the exercise it provided but also for the beneficial effect on the young participants.

......

The shorter and certainly more scenic rail journey from Leeds to Carlisle is to take the Trans-Pennine Express. This infrequent service runs on a single track that crosses the Pennines, runs north through the western edge of the Yorkshire Dales National Park and then follows the valley of the River Eden to Carlisle. Just north of Horton-in-Ribblesdale, the line crosses the long Ribblehead Viaduct.

Jack had been told to bring trainers and sports gear with him. It was only as the train was slowly crossing this famous feat of Victorian engineering that it dawned on him why the interviews were being held at an army training centre just outside Carlisle; the fitness of the applicants would almost certainly be put to the test on a formidable obstacle course.

"Thank goodness I'm really fit and should be able to hold my own against almost everybody," he mused.

......

He reported to the camp guardhouse at 11:50, ten minutes before his midday interview, and was immediately taken to a nearby hut. A friendly girl in civilian clothes produced a cup of coffee and asked him to wait before disappearing into the adjacent room.

Five minutes later, she returned. "You may go in now. I'll look after your bag," she said and ushered him through the door into a sparse room containing only a desk, two wooden chairs and a large waste-paper basket. Despite his nervousness, Jack could not help noticing that the latter held the remains of a thick telephone directory neatly torn in half parallel to its spine.

A middle-aged man in a dark suit sat behind the desk, empty except for Jack's application letter and CV. He stood up and shook hands before gesturing to the chair facing the desk.

"Please sit down," he said. "I'm John Palmer and I've been charged with conducting the interviews today. This venue is not ideal but we needed the use of part of the obstacle course for a couple of hours and the British Army is only too pleased to get a little extra income."

Without further preamble, he proceeded to probe Jack's background, nodding encouragingly from time to time. He was particularly interested in the fact that Jack could speak passable German, having learned it from a Swiss student he had befriended at Sheffield University. The latter had spent nine months in Sheffield on an exchange from the University of Berne.

After twenty minutes, Mr Palmer appeared satisfied and said: "I've taken the liberty of speaking to both your referees by telephone. Your university tutor speaks very highly of you, I'm glad to say, and the manager of the boy's fitness club was even more effusive in his praise."

"Unfortunately, I can't give you any details about the job itself until you've completed the obstacle course," he continued. "You're the fourth and final applicant to attempt it. My secretary, Amy, will take you to get changed and then introduce you to the army sergeant in charge of the course. We've selected five of the most appropriate sections for you to complete as fast and as accurately as you can. But take care; if you make a mistake during any stage, he'll send you back to the beginning of that section."

The man rose to his feet and called for Amy. "Good luck!" he said, looking as if he really meant it.

Thus encouraged, Jack followed Amy out of the building.
......

About an hour later, still quite flushed after all his exertion even though he had had a quick shower, Jack found himself following Amy once more. She led him to a room that appeared to be attached to the officers' mess. A cold buffet was set out at one end of a large table and she hurried over to remove the cling film from the various dishes.

Two other people were already in the room; John Palmer was by the door waiting to greet him and a tall girl wearing a smart grey suit stood on the far side of the room looking out of the window at the activity taking place on the parade ground. The dull thud of boots and bellows of a sergeant major penetrated the double glazing.

"Well done Jack!" John said warmly. "You managed a much faster time over the obstacle course than our other two male candidates. However, Lucy here," he gestured to the girl by the window, "amazed us all, not least the sergeant in charge, by beating your time by nine seconds! I've sent the other two men away, saying we'd be in touch with them later, because I very much hope you and Lucy will find that you can work well together."

He called across the room: "Lucy, show Jack what you did earlier; it certainly impressed me."

Without a word, the girl picked up a telephone directory that had been lying on the window sill beside her and turned towards them. Gripping the top of the volume firmly with both hands, she gave a slight shrug and tore it apart in one smooth seemingly effortless action. Placing the two halves neatly back on the window sill, she crossed the room towards them.

"You see what I mean?" John asked. "That directory was well over two inches thick!"

"To say I'm impressed would be an understatement," Jack responded. "Lucy's obviously amazingly strong. It'll be a privilege to work with her."

"It just needs a little practice," the girl said, speaking for the first time. "I'll show you the technique if you like and then we could have a competition."

Although her offer sounded quite friendly, the accompanying smile conveyed the impression that she did not rate his chance of success very highly.

"Thank you; I look forward to it." Jack's words emerged almost automatically.

At close quarters, Lucy's neat oval face, framed by rich brown hair that fell well below her shoulders, was strangely attractive in a way he could not define; all he knew was that it was almost as fascinating as her remarkable strength.

"We've got things to discuss," John interposed. "Lucy, shake hands with your new partner and then we'll have some food. I'll explain what the job entails as we eat."

Lucy took Jack's offered hand. Her hand closed over his like a vice. He had never felt such a powerful grip and he must have winced because John chuckled and called out from the table: "Lucy, let him go; he already knows how strong you are."

The girl gave another superior smile, released her crushing grip and turned towards the table.

"I'm glad you're on my side!" Jack exclaimed with a laugh, trying to make light of the episode even though his hand would take several minutes to recover.

After everyone had helped themselves from the food on offer, John sat at the head of the table and gestured for Lucy and Jack to sit together on one side with Amy facing them, notepad at her side.

The only drink on the table was water and Amy poured glasses for everyone.

"Only water, I'm afraid," their host apologised. "We need to keep clear heads. Some coffee will arrive later."

Everyone ate in silence for a few minutes and then he began to explain the task for which the two young people had been selected.

Chapter 2: Task Explained

"From time to time," John said slowly, picking his words with care, "museums in this country discover that something in their possession turns out to have been stolen from a previous owner. The case that concerns us here involves the Bodleian Library in Oxford and a small manuscript dating from 1721.

"Research into recently discovered documents by an Oxford postgraduate has proved conclusively that this unique and very valuable manuscript was once in the possession of a wealthy Jewish family. It contains a selection of Old Testament psalms and was presented to the Russian Tsar, Peter the Great, by his wife, Catherine, to commemorate the final establishment of the Russian Empire in 1721. The illuminated frontispiece is a work of art in its own right and contains a personal message from Catherine to her husband. The gift was intended for Peter's private devotions and is therefore quite small: about the size of a hardback novel.

"The manuscript was confiscated by the Nazi Party early in 1936 when the persecution of Jews really got going. A few months later, the family managed to escape to Switzerland. Soon after settling in their new country, they had a son who eventually became an extremely prosperous business man and now lives in retirement in an alpine village in the Bernese Oberland. He was delighted when the Bodleian informed him of the discovery.

"The Library contains a museum and initially asked to be allowed to continue to display the manuscript as a loan, but the man insisted that it be returned. He said he did not want to use a security company specializing in the shipment of valuable items and was prepared to cover the expense of conducting the transfer in extreme secrecy. As the result, my small company has been hired to do the job. People like us are sometimes known as "fixers"!"

John paused to eat after requesting Amy to slip out to the kitchen and ask for the coffee and hot water to be brought in fifteen minutes.

While she was absent he continued: "As it turns out, all this secrecy could be much more important than we first thought. The Director of the Bodleian now suspects that there may be somebody on his staff acting as an informer for the Russian mafia!"

Even ice-cool Lucy looked surprised at this revelation and Jack felt a surge of excitement. John, however, continued as if he had not delivered something of a bombshell.

"It's common knowledge that the mafia launder their ill-gotten gains by buying things like jewellery and paintings on the open market. However, they are all too ready to steal such things as well. It has occurred to them that old manuscripts can sometimes be very valuable; hence their potential interest in the Bodleian Library."

John looked at Lucy and Jack for a moment before continuing.

"Our idea is for you to appear to be a young couple spending a delightful week hiking and trail running in the Swiss Alps. You'll be supplied with British Airways tickets from London Heathrow to Basle Mulhouse airport, about four miles from the centre of Basle, and train tickets from there to Interlaken.

"In outline, the plan is this: you'll start by spending four nights in a small hotel or guesthouse of your choice in a village not far from Interlaken. During that time, you can acclimatize yourselves to the altitude by hiking and running in the surrounding area. Then you'll move base for another four nights to Adelboden, about 30 miles from Interlaken. Our retired businessman lives just outside Kandersteg in the neighbouring valley.

"I've discovered that there's a 16 km trek over the mountain pass between the two valleys, estimated to take about seven hours. On a date to be arranged, you'll undertake this journey in time to be having refreshments in a particular café by one-thirty in the afternoon. Here the package containing the manuscript will be discretely exchanged for a receipt and then you'll be free to return the way you came before it gets dark: hence the need to be ultra-fit. Only use public transport to get back to Adelboden if it becomes essential for some reason. Your daily trail running will act as excellent camouflage for this one vital clandestine trip."

"If we run where it's safe to do so, it should be possible to halve the estimated hiking time," Lucy volunteered. "Speaking for myself, I'm quite happy to run for miles and even jog up a steep gradient if necessary."

The glance she gave Jack indicated doubt in his ability to keep up such a pace but he hardly noticed because he had his own information to impart.

"As it happens, I have a Swiss friend whose parents run a guesthouse in Wilderswil, a village about two miles from Interlaken on the narrow-gauge railway into the Jungfrau region. I stayed there with him about two years ago. He's working in the USA at the moment but I'm sure his parents would be happy for us to stay there; we'd have to pay of course."

John nodded approvingly at them, rather like a teacher acknowledging prize pupils. "Everything seems to be coming together very nicely," he said.

......

Amy returned at this point looking rather flustered. "I'm sorry to have been so long," she said. "The kitchen denied all knowledge of our having included tea and coffee in our lunch order. It was only when I pointed out that the request must have got through because we already had cups and tea bags on the table that they reluctantly accepted they were at fault. Hopefully something should arrive fairly soon!"

"Thanks Amy; I don't know what I'd do without you," John sighed.

Turning to Lucy and Jack, he explained: "Our company is actually extremely small; apart from the two us, there's only my senior partner, Ian, and he's not far from retirement. Failure to complete this job successfully could well be the end of us!"

A worried frown appeared on his face before he shrugged off this unhappy thought and carried on with his instructions.

"Restrict yourselves to aircraft cabin bags and don't forget that the UV level in the mountains will be high even when the sun is not out, so take sunglasses and sun cream and remember that the size limit for anything in a tube or bottle is 75ml. You'll also need small rucksacks, or similar, to carry water etc. on your outings, not to mention the precious manuscript that mustn't leave your possession at any time. Anyway, the fine details can be worked out later. What's more important now is to get your first three weeks of training organised; I'm hoping you can start very soon."

He looked at Lucy first to get her reaction.

"I could get back here as early as next Wednesday," she replied.

"It's the same for me," Jack added quickly. There really was very little for him to do except buy two more running T-shirts; he already had some excellent shorts, footgear and a light-weight windproof jacket.

John was clearly pleased. "That's excellent!" he said. "Amy will give you both £200 to cover incidental expenses, your fares today and returning to Carlisle next Wednesday. Come to our small office near the town centre."

Thus prompted, Amy passed two envelopes across the table while John produced two business cards from his wallet. "I'll be waiting for you at this address at three o'clock. Then we'll drive to the hamlet of Terregles in Scotland, about three miles west of Dumfries, where Ian is allowing you the use of his retirement bungalow purchased a mere two months ago.

The previous owner left quite a well-equipped fitness studio in the garden that'll be excellent for your purposes and the surrounding countryside should provide good opportunities for running. After about two weeks, you can use his old camper van to visit the Scottish Highlands to do some trail running in the mountains."

John smiled at them. He looked pleased with all his careful planning.

"I'll only keep in touch at a distance but there's a widow in the village, a Mrs McCready, who'll do your laundry once a week and cook a main meal each evening – Ian says she's an excellent cook, having spent two weekends there already. She even brings in fresh vegetables from her garden. Otherwise, you'll be looking after yourselves."

The coffee arrived at this point and Jack and Lucy found themselves standing together with their cups at the window where she had stood earlier. Outside, a number of new recruits were being put through their paces. A drill sergeant had them all face down doing push-ups and appeared to be driving them to exhaustion.

"I regularly do 50 push-ups," Lucy said quietly. She did not appear to be boasting but merely stating a fact.

There and then, Jack decided not to allow himself to be disconcerted by anything she said but thankful that he had a really tough companion for what might well turn out to be an arduous and possibly dangerous task. Anyway, she intrigued him in more ways than one.

Then he became aware that she was speaking again.

"I've been into fitness for almost nine years now – gymnastics, long-distance running and several sports including cross-fit – so I'm familiar with most types of exercise equipment. Would you have any objection if I set out an exercise plan for us once I know what's available?"

"With all your experience, I'm more than happy for you to organise our regime," Jack responded.

His ready acceptance of her proposal resulted in the first sign of a slight thaw in Lucy's attitude towards him. She looked pleased and remarked: "Progress is usually better when people train together and encourage each other."

Jack turned to her and held out his hand. This time she responded with a normal firm grip.

John appeared beside them. "I can see you two are getting on well," he said. "Let me run you back to Carlisle station in my car. Amy can finish clearing up here."

......

It was on the short journey that John revealed a little more information.

"I'm going to book your outbound flight for the first Wednesday in June and return eight days later. Hopefully, the guesthouse you mentioned in Wilderswil can take you for the first four nights and you can use Google Maps to list two or three small hotels or guesthouses in Adelboden. But don't book anything; it should be fairly easy to find accommodation so early in the summer season and you'll be paying with cash for the sake of anonymity.

"I'll fix up your visit to Kandersteg for the following Tuesday and let you know which café or restaurant has been selected. At 13:30 a trusted household servant wearing a salmon-pink shirt will be inside the café at a table near the back. Sit at a table near the door if possible, order your refreshments and leave the manuscript tucked inside a folded newspaper on the table beside you. When it's safe to do so, the man will pass you on his way out and remove the newspaper, leaving an envelope containing the receipt in its place.

"The latter will eventually have to be given to the Bodleian to satisfy their book-keeping. The Director and I are still working out how you're going to collect the manuscript from Oxford in the first place. It's all rather complicated because he doesn't know who the rotten apple is, or even if there definitely is one!"

A few minutes later, they stopped outside the station. "See you both next Wednesday afternoon. Safe travelling!" John said, giving a friendly wave as he drove off.

It turned out that Lucy had half an hour to wait for the next train to Lancaster and Jack a little longer.

"Before I offer you a cup of tea or coffee, it might be sensible to find out the times of our trains next Wednesday," Jack suggested.

Lucy nodded. "I'll return your hospitality when we meet back here prior to going to.....," she said, determined not to be beholden to him, as her hand felt around in a pocket for John's business card. "I hope I haven't lost the address of John's office," she muttered.

"I've got his card in my wallet," Jack reassured her, gazing at his new partner for rather longer than was polite. To cover his mistake, he said the first thing that came into his head: "Your jacket has a surprising number of pockets."

Caught off her guard, Lucy gave a wry smile. "Most of them are fake. Even women wearing business suits must maintain the sleek look at all costs: no unsightly bulges allowed!"

In fact, her suit fitted perfectly, giving no indication that inside was a body of steel.

......

It was with considerable pleasure that Lucy looked back on a very successful day as her train drew away from the platform. Although her new job would only last for five weeks, she could hardly believe that she was going to be paid to run in the Swiss Alps of all places! She loved running – the tougher the terrain the better – and almost any activity demanding strength and endurance in which she could delight in demonstrating that she was the equal of any man.

One thing she regretted; she would not be alone. It was annoying because she liked her own company and could easily manage what appeared to be a simple delivery unaided, mafia or no mafia! As it was, she was lumbered with a male companion, although at least he had had the sense to readily agree to let her organize their training sessions. She would really put Jack to the test and see if he was as tough as he appeared. It was surprising that he had not responded to her vicelike handshake; she usually found that male pride resulted in a vain attempt to respond.

She sat back and gazed out at the passing countryside with satisfaction. Then a strange thought crossed her mind: "I wonder what Jack thinks of me?" The odd thing about it was that she hardly ever cared what other people thought of her.

......

As it happened, Jack was also looking out of a carriage window but his train was only just leaving Carlisle. He too was looking back on the day with satisfaction. To spend eight days in Switzerland, and be paid to do so, was almost too good to be true. Not only that, but it would be in the company of a quite amazing girl.

Hopefully, her early antagonism would continue to dissipate when she saw that he was determined to live up to her high athletic standards and work hard to make up where he was lacking. He could not help being fascinated by her and looked forward to seeing her in her exercise gear; no doubt she would look fantastic.

Chapter 3: Training in Progress

Jack would get his wish fulfilled soon after half past six the following Thursday morning, although he would have preferred it not to be quite so early.

They had arrived in John's car early the previous evening at an attractive three-bedroom bungalow in Terregles with the absolute minimum of things needed for over a month away squeezed into their backpacks.

John had returned to Carlisle after an excellent meal provided by Mrs McCready, leaving Lucy and Jack to explore the pleasant garden and all-important studio.

The wooden building was surprisingly large and had several windows. A small rack of dumb-bells stood by the door and five pieces of apparatus, one of which looked suspiciously like an instrument of torture to Jack's untrained eye, surrounded an exercise mat in the centre of the floor. He recognised the pull-up bar and taller exercise tower, rowing machine and adjustable exercise bench, but would have to wait for his new trainer to explain the intricacies of the mystery object.

"The place is rather better than I expected," Lucy admitted. "We can do a fair amount with the equipment in here and I can plan some floor exercises to fill in the gaps. I'm determined to put us both through full-body workouts all morning every morning."

Jack pointed to the instrument of torture. "What on earth is that?" he asked.

"It goes by the initials GHD and is designed to develop glutes, hams and lower back," she replied, adding, when he looked mystified: "Your glutes are your buttocks and your hamstrings are the rear leg muscles above the knee joint: the counterpart of your thighs.

"I'll demonstrate how everything works first thing tomorrow. You can have a go on each device until you get the

16

hang of it. Then we can really get going in earnest. I'll work out a sensible sequence and fit in weight training and floor exercises at appropriate points, the idea being to exercise different muscle groups in turn. I'll gradually increase the time spent on each activity as the days pass; for example, we may start with ten pull-ups but gradually increase to about twenty."

"I'm quite happy to start with twenty," Jack said, hoping to impress her.

"Believe me; you'll be glad to limit the repetitions when we go through the whole cycle of exercises almost nonstop," Lucy replied.

He was pleased to see that her rather supercilious attitude had been supplanted by a firm determination to prepare them both for the challenging task ahead.

......

So now here he was at 6:35 on Thursday morning, still bleary-eyed, standing beside her in the studio for a pre-breakfast session.

"We need to warm up first," Lucy said. "Stand on the mat facing me and copy what I do."

This instruction cleared Jack's head instantly; he needed no encouragement to gaze at her.

A pale blue tank top and skimpy black shorts did little to conceal a perfectly proportioned and beautifully muscled body, complemented by the appealingly attractive face framed by rich espresso-brown hair that he had so admired a few days earlier, although the latter was now considerably shorter.

"She must have cut it ready for action," he thought, looking on with fascination as she lifted her hands and deftly swept the hair back to secure it in a ponytail that fell just short of shoulder level.

Even such a straightforward action somehow conveyed the sense that she was in total control of her movements and possessed the latent power to surge into action the instant it was required. It was no longer difficult to understand how she

17

had completed the army obstacle course in such good time or the apparently effortless way in which she had torn a telephone directory in half.

Although this amazing girl clearly got her remarkable strength from quality rather than quantity, her exercise regime and sheer determination had resulted in muscles appropriately described by the recently popular description "ripped". Anyway, they were most certainly rippling superbly before Jack's admiring eyes as she performed the first warm-up exercise.

......

"You're not paying attention!" Lucy's sharp rebuke rang out. "At the moment I'm the only one warming up; you're just standing there daydreaming."

"Sorry! I'm still half asleep," Jack replied sheepishly and hastened to pay careful attention and follow every movement as closely possible.

Lucy was obviously determined to carry out their assignment successfully and was not the sort of girl who would put up with any slacking on his part or, even worse, amorous attention. Were she to refuse to have anything more to do with him, he remembered John's words about "hoping" that the two of them would find they could work well together. He dare not risk the possibility of being sacked at this early stage and never seeing her again.

"OK, now for some serious exercise," Lucy said after a couple of minutes, stepping towards the rack of dumb-bells. "We'll take two each and do some weight training."

She handed him a couple of 5 kg dumb-bells and looked for two for herself. "That's annoying: this rack only has two of each weight. I'll have to use 6 kg ones."

"That's the equivalent of about 13 lb!" Jack exclaimed but then remembered the telephone directory and wished he had kept his mouth shut.

Lucy did not comment but gave an almost imperceptible smile before carrying on with her instructions.

"In the first exercise, keeping our backs straight, we'll lift the bells vertically above our heads from shoulder level and lower again." She thrust the dumb-bells up as if they were almost weightless and then lowered them until her hands were close to the front of her shoulders. "We'll do 15 repetitions. Join in with me now and I'll count."

Jack copied her with his lighter weights, wondering whether it would be chivalrous to offer to swap in future. He decided it would be wiser not to do so.

It was not long before the next set of instructions was issued. "Now stand with your legs apart, bend forward slightly at the waist with your arms straight down in front of you, draw your abs in tight and, keeping your arms straight, lift the weights directly up in front of you. Try to reach shoulder level. Hold that position for a second and then lower. We'll repeat 15 times. Ready?" She looked across at Jack who grinned and nodded.

"Up...one...two...down...up...one...two...down...up...one... two......"

At last she stopped. Jack's bells felt as if the cast iron had morphed into lead but he dare not complain because the girl beside him seemed quite happy with her heavier ones.

After not more than half a minute's recovery time, Lucy stood with her legs together and arms straight down at her sides.

"Just hold the dumb-bells like this to give us extra weight," she said. "The idea is to exercise our core and legs by forcing both thighs to work hard to hold us in what's called the lunge position. We step forward with one leg and, keeping that foot flat on the floor, drop down so that our thigh is as near horizontal as possible. As a result, the other leg is forced to bend towards the kneeling position. Watch me."

She lunged forward with her right leg until her thigh was horizontal and braced to hold her in that position; at the same time, her left knee came within two inches of the floor, leaving only her toes in contact with the ground. She remained frozen in that position.

"Look at my thighs," she ordered, not that Jack needed any encouragement to do so. "It's probably obvious, even from where you're standing, that they're under stress."

"Yes indeed," Jack agreed, but could not help thinking that they were doing the job remarkably easily with no sign of a tremor.

She stood up again. "We'll lunge with alternate legs and stay down for four seconds each time. Follow me now with six double steps, starting with the right leg. Go!"

Almost to his surprise, Jack managed quite well, although he was thankful Lucy did not delay as long in the lunge position as she had during her demonstration.

Another very short rest was permitted. Lucy was perspiring slightly now but otherwise still looked as fresh as a daisy.

"Finally, we'll finish with some bicep curls. Start with your arms slightly bent and then continue to lift your forearms until the bells almost touch your shoulders. Lower again but don't let your arms straighten completely. It should be easy with these modest weights and so I won't bother to count; just follow me."

When Lucy stopped at last, she said: "Put the bells back while you have a short rest and I explain the final exercise before breakfast. We don't have long because, this being our first morning, Mrs McCready is in the kitchen kindly preparing fried eggs and bacon for us. Expect boiled eggs tomorrow when I prepare breakfast!"

Jack joined her at the adjustable abdominal bench. As the name implied, it was a padded bench or plank that could be inclined at different angles. At the higher end were two pairs of padded projections a short distance apart.

"I tried out something similar to this when I was about sixteen; a friend of mine had been given one for his birthday," he said. "However, please demonstrate."

Lucy climbed on and bent her legs over the lower pair of pads and tucked her feet under the upper ones so that both legs were held firmly in an inverted V-shape. Lying back on the bench, she crossed her arms over her chest, paused for a moment and then smoothly curled up until her chest was almost vertical.

She held this position while she explained: "This version of the crunch is brilliant for strengthening the lower abs. It's important not to bend your head forward as you curl up because that will strain your neck. Let your abs do all the work and breathe correctly; exhale as you sit up, hold the position for a second, and then inhale as you go down. Don't allow your head to touch the bench, keep your abs taut and sit up again almost immediately. Watch me demonstrate for a minute."

Lucy lowered herself and proceeded to curl up at least ten times. Jack watched in admiration as her superb abs contracted and stretched, giving no indication of being worked particularly hard.

"Now it's your turn," she said. "I usually make it harder by holding a weight on my chest but you need to start with the straightforward version first."

Jack got into the rhythm of the exercise more easily than he had expected and even managed to achieve twenty crunches before lying back on the bench to recover.

"Well done," Lucy said as he climbed off. "But be warned, I'll gradually make the bench steeper!"

......

After breakfast and a 30-minute break to let their food settle, they were back in the studio. Lucy went straight to the GHD. It consisted of a short frame with a pair of padded rollers at one end, a small kneeling pad in the centre and a single much larger thickly padded cylinder at the other end.

"This small pad is just to help you get on," Lucy said as she knelt on it to push her feet between the rollers so that her toes pointed downwards. Her thighs were now pressing against the inside of the large cylinder with her torso vertical.

She folded her arms across her chest and slowly leant forward to roll over the cylinder, with her lower stomach pressing into its padded surface, until her body was straight and parallel to the floor. Her upper body now had no support from below.

"My rear muscles are working hard to hold me in this position and they're about to be forced to work even harder," she said. "Put your hand on my butt and feel what happens when I dip down by 45 degrees and then pull myself back above the horizontal position."

"I can't do that!" Jack exclaimed, taken completely by surprise.

"Why not?" she queried. "I only want you to see how good the apparatus is at exercising the glutes etc. Of course, if you do anything like this without my permission, I'll flatten you!"

Jack thought he heard her give a very faint chuckle as he cautiously reached out, only to be amazed at the hardness of the muscle that greeted the palm of his hand. Even so, there was a stirring within him; it was the first time he had ever touched this part of a girl's anatomy, let alone one so attractive. But he was even more impressed when she dipped down and came back up again until her body formed a graceful upward arc; it felt as if her glutes had become liquid steel as they stretched and contracted.

Lucy counted as she continued to dip down and come back up again. It was obviously becoming gradually harder because, as she muttered "fifteen" through clenched teeth, she grabbed the sides to the cylinder to help her return to the vertical position and extricate herself from the apparatus.

"I thought the thing resembled some sort of torture device; self torture in this case!" Jack remarked as she stood beside him, stretching to relieve the tension.

"I'll increase the distance between the rollers and cylinder because your legs are slightly longer than mine," she said, fiddling with some handles. "OK, now try it out."

Jack managed to maintain the horizontal position fairly easily, but, after seven dips, he was struggling. Lucy took pity on him and helped him extricate himself.

He rubbed his sore limbs. "I'll never manage many of those!" he exclaimed.

"You'll be surprised; by the middle of next week, you'll be doing double that," she said confidently.

"Rest for three minutes and then we'll start our first complete round of exercises. We'll do some pull-ups first. You use the pull-up bar and I'll take the bar on the tower; eight dead-hang pull-ups with our palms facing forwards, then a brief pause before reversing hands for the same number of chin-ups."

She paused while they jumped up and adjusted their grip. "OK? Get set. Go!"

She called out a steady timing as they worked away together. This was an exercise that Jack knew well; he had set up a bar in the small garage attached to his ground floor flat and used it frequently. Two pull-up bars were also amongst the modest amount of kit possessed by the boys' club where he helped out every week.

They dropped off their respective bars and stood for a few seconds to regain their breath.

"I can see you're good at these," Lucy said. "Later this week, we'll have a competition. We can even try the one-arm version to see how strong you really are!" She looked delighted at the prospect. "Anyway, before we move on, I'll just demonstrate something else that can be done on the horizontal bar in the tower. In fact, I'll continue to do it while you use the rowing machine for a short time. Don't worry; I'll still be keeping an eye on you!"

She sprang up, gripped the bar and pulled herself up so that she could hook her legs over it and hang upside down. Crossing her forearms over her chest, she then proceeded to use the power of her abs to crunch up until her arms almost reached thighs of steel holding her legs locked in position.

After five repetitions, she stopped for a moment to say: "You can try this in a day or two after you've done more time on the abdominal bench; start rowing now while I continue with some more."

Jack obediently rowed at a rapid pace, letting his own thighs thrust him powerfully back on the machine whilst he dwelt on the fact that this amazing girl appeared to be carrying on crunching with very little effort.

......

It turned out to be a challenging and enjoyable morning. Lucy blended in a series of floor exercises at appropriate points, including push-ups where she insisted on placing a heavy dumbbell on Jack's back to increase the difficulty. An excellent instructor, she pushed him hard but certainly did not spare herself.

By one o'clock, they were more than ready for a break and shared the task of preparing a simple lunch before sitting down thankfully at the kitchen table.

"Before we go for our run this afternoon, I'll look at the map of the area that John left on the hall table," Lucy said. "I want to include Dumfries on our route. It's only three or four miles away and I'd like to get some wholemeal bread. Mrs McCready has only got in white bread; wholemeal will be much better for us."

......

Three hours later, after a run of over 15 miles, they were back at the same table having a cup of tea. After such a long and energetic morning, Jack was pleased to have managed the distance quite comfortably, although Lucy had been content to set a modest steady pace of about seven miles an hour. The journey had been considerably improved, however, by the pleasure of watching her delightful rear view.

They were on their second cup of tea when Mrs McCready bustled in to begin preparing the evening meal.

She was delighted to find that Lucy had already peeled and cut up some potatoes and carrots.

"That's very kind of you dear," she said to Lucy. "I was hoping to get away in good time because a friend is popping in this evening for a hot drink and nice chat."

She put the vegetables on to boil and got a frying pan out of the cupboard. "You're having fried lamb's liver and onions with a little bacon to give extra flavour."

She noticed the slight grimace on Jack's expressive face and immediately discerned its cause.

"Don't worry young man; I guarantee you'll like liver the way I cook it," she said. "My husband, bless him, was exactly the same when we married but it was not long before he was happily eating it at least once a week!"

When she placed loaded plates in front of the two hungry young people half an hour later, Jack took a tentative mouthful. Chewing cautiously, a big smile spread over his face.

"You were right, Mrs McCready, this is really good!" he said in surprise.

The old woman smiled with pleasure and was even more pleased when Lucy, who had been tucking in with gusto, said: "You go now, Mrs McCready, and have a lovely evening. Jack and I will wash up."

"Thank you, dear, that's very thoughtful of you, but please call me Mary in future."

25

She took off her apron. "For desert, there's a choice of several different fruit yogurts in the 'fridge," she said as she opened the back door. "Goodnight!"

......

Given Lucy's speed and efficiency at the kitchen sink, it did not take long before everything was spick and span, but it was only whilst hanging up the tea-towel used to dry the dishes that Jack finally plucked up courage to issue the invitation he had been mulling over since the start of the meal.

"Lucy, as a thank-you for demonstrating all the equipment and planning our exercise regime, would you like to stroll down to the pub for a drink?"

He waited in suspense as she rinsed out the washing-up bowl and upended it in the sink to drain.

"I accept, but under two conditions: you limit yourself to one pint of beer or similar and we have an arm-wrestling contest across the kitchen table afterwards."

Surprised but pleased, Jack nodded. "One pint has always been my limit and I was quite good at arm-wrestling once upon a time."

"Excellent, I look forward to the contest!" Lucy gave him a challenging glance for a moment before her face softened. "But thanks for the invitation. I'll get my anorak."

Chapter 4: Making Friends

Although initially rather cool and aloof, Lucy became more relaxed as the evening progressed. It probably helped that she was pleased when Jack matched her choice of drink and brought two half-pints of lager to their small table.

"I expect you're more of a beer man; I'm sorry if I've cramped your style," she said.

Jack shook his head. "No, I sometimes prefer cold lager, especially after a hot day, and I'm restricting myself to half because I want to be ready for our competition."

"I'm naturally competitive as you've no doubt guessed, but my main reason for suggesting arm-wrestling is that it's excellent exercise when the people involved are well matched, as I think we will be," Lucy said. "You've probably also realized by now that I'm only happy when doing something physical!"

It suddenly dawned on her that this last sentence was open to misinterpretation and her face turned bright red.

Trying to spare her embarrassment, Jack jumped in with the first thing that came into his head. "As far as I'm concerned, I couldn't have a better trainer. Anyway, I'm looking forward to arm-wrestling; it'll be great fun!"

Lucy said nothing but looked at him with the friendliest smile he had seen so far.

As he basked in that smile he could not help reflecting on how she had changed since the interview day.

It was almost as if she had read his thoughts. "I'm sorry about my attitude towards you when we first met; I tend to get too full of myself and it was made worse by the fact that John set me up."

She looked at him almost apologetically. "You see, I was sent on the obstacle course as soon as I arrived and so, at the later interview, John complimented me on my fitness and agility and asked what else I could do. Seeing two telephone directories in the waste basket, I foolishly offered to tear one in half. He was so impressed that the rest of the interview was a doddle!

"It was only when Amy showed me into the dining-room that he surprised me by producing the second directory and told me to stand by the window and be ready to do it again. It soon transpired, of course, that he intended to jolt you into treating me as an equal partner and not as some frail female who would be a hindrance. The consequence of showing off like that for the second time left me with an inflated ego!"

Jack reached out and briefly touched the hand beside her glass. "I guess I would have felt exactly the same had I torn two directories apart, especially as you made it look so easy! I'm not surprised about your crushing handshake either; a moment earlier you had gripped the top of that directory so hard I could even see it being compressed!"

Lucy did not reply but gave him another smile.

By now, Jack had detected that his new companion's self-assured exterior concealed an intensely private and rather vulnerable person. This realization brought out a protective streak in his kind nature and he determined to support and guard her in any way he could.

......

After returning to the house, Lucy had the foresight to put a folded towel on the kitchen table to make it less painful for their elbows. Fortunately, the table was small enough for their raised right hands to meet comfortably in the centre and their left hands to grip the opposite edges for stability.

"I'll just align our shoulders, elbows and arms and then we'll be ready to go," Lucy said, making the adjustments with her left hand before gripping the table again. "I suggest we count down...three, two, one...go! Do you want to do it or shall I?"

"You can," Jack said, bracing himself.

"OK, take up the strain...three, two, one...go!"

Both of them reacted with equal speed and their hands remained locked in the vertical position with barely perceptible movement either side.

Jack, for his part, was trying to pace himself because he had witnessed the strength of his opponent and deduced that his only hope of success was to hold on until she began to tire and then try to summon sufficient strength to overcome her. In the event, however, her endurance turned out to be just as impressive as her strength and so their stalemate lasted for well over two minutes. Eventually, to his dismay, it was his arm, not hers, that began to exhibit the tell-tale tremor.

Lucy detected this almost immediately and skilfully manoeuvred her forearm to hook her wrist around his, thus giving her greater leverage. Jack watched helplessly as her superb bicep rose even further and his hand was forced slowly back and pinned down.

She released him with a cry of triumph and massaged her arm while she waited for him to recover.

"This is turning into a real battle! Shall we say best of five instead of the usual three?" she said, raising her left hand in challenge.

"OK," Jack agreed. "I'm certainly not finished yet!"

"Good," she muttered as their hands locked again. "Take the strain...three, two, one...go!"

They struggled for almost as long as before but the outcome was different. To Jack's considerable relief, it was Lucy who found herself desperately trying to hold on as her hand was forced to the table.

"I'm impressed," was all she said as they locked right hands for the second time.

Jack grinned but remained silent; he did not want to count his chickens before they hatched.

His caution turned out to be sensible because it was not long before they were clasping right hands for the third time with the score at two all.

"OK, this is the decider. Get ready to be defeated!" Lucy said, making deliberate eye contact and trying to intimidate him.

"In your dreams!" Jack replied, returning her gaze and sounding more confident than he felt; not only had she won twice already with her right arm but she was betraying very little sign of stress.

The final battle lasted for almost as long as the previous four rounds put together. Neither combatant was prepared to yield, although their clenched hands swayed back and forth by several inches as first one and then the other began to gain the upper hand but then lacked the power to carry it through.

In the end, their arms shaking with weariness, they looked at each other and agreed to call the match a draw.

Jack slowly got to his feet, took a rather surprised Lucy by the hand and led her into the sitting room where they collapsed on the settee to recover.

A couple of minutes later, Lucy chuckled quietly. "That was the best contest I've ever had and quite brilliant exercise for us both. After doing that a few times, together with all the studio sessions and running, we should be honed to perfection in about two week's time when we go trail-running in the Highlands."

"You look honed to perfection already," Jack said as he struggled off the low settee. "Stay there and I'll bring you a bedtime drink. What do you fancy?"

Lucy grinned up at him. "There's always room for improvement. Decaf please – I think I saw some in the cupboard."

Jack returned with two steaming mugs of coffee a few minutes later, put one on the coffee table beside Lucy and sat down opposite her in an armchair.

"Did John tell you when he wanted us to take Ian's camper van to the Highlands? I looked it over this afternoon and was surprised at its good condition – he called it old!"

"Judging by his smart new Audi, he probably calls anything old if made more than three years ago!" she replied. "But to return to your question, he wants us to leave on Wednesday week to spend four nights at the caravan site Amy's booked for us in Morvich, about 60 miles from Fort William. That means we only have another twelve whole days here, plus maybe one after we return on the Sunday."

Jack looked thoughtful. "It all depends on when John wants us to take the train south from Carlisle," he said. "We're due to fly to Switzerland from London Heathrow the following Wednesday and we've got to collect the precious manuscript from the Bodleian Library in Oxford the day before. The schedule is beginning to look extremely tight. I hope he's thought of a convincing reason why we should visit Oxford on our way to Heathrow: it's not exactly the most direct route!"

"I only hope our involvement is not discovered." Lucy sounded uncharacteristically worried.

Jack shook his head. "Even if the suspected mole in the Bodleian finds out the name of John's company, we should still be safe provided we've already set off and are no longer in contact with him."

"I'm probably worrying because I'm tired," Lucy said. "I need to recharge my batteries; I'm off to bed. Goodnight!"

......

The days at Terregles passed quickly. Under Lucy's careful guidance, Jack's performance on the apparatus and floor exercises improved rapidly and he even achieved no less than 15 repetitions on the GHD apparatus, as she had predicted. She even showed him how lie face up and do a version of the crunch.

"Flexible athletes can arch right back over the padded cylinder and achieve a really wide range of motion; brilliant for abs and a lot more!" she said.

When she demonstrated by doing several amazing semi-circular crunches, Jack was lost in admiration. What made

31

things difficult was that he was now well past the mere admiration stage and becoming increasingly attracted to her as a person. In fact, he was falling in love but dare not show it.

......

A session of arm-wrestling took place most evenings. They were so closely matched that a fifth round was invariably necessary, but, except for that memorable first evening when exhaustion had forced a draw, it always produced a winner. Although Jack usually triumphed, Lucy sometimes overcame him by sheer guts and determination.

One evening, towards the end of their time at the bungalow, Lucy suggested an alternative to arm-wrestling as they walked back from their regular visit to the pub. It had been a lovely sunny day and the cool of the evening was particularly inviting

"Have I mentioned that I tried a little wrestling before I got caught up in the excitement and challenge of cross-fit?" she asked.

"No, I don't think so," Jack replied, wondering what was coming next.

"If we take the exercise mat out on to that patch of turf just beyond the studio, I could teach you a couple of wrestling throws. They might come in useful if faced by a mafia thug or two!"

She chuckled at the thought of this highly unlikely event but continued quickly. "Anyway, it will be good sport and that part of the garden is not overlooked."

"I'm happy to do whatever you suggest," Jack said, feeling excited by the thought of physical contact. So far, she had not even linked arms with him on the way to or from the pub.

......

The secluded garden was pleasantly cool. After changing back into exercise gear, the two young people faced each other across the mat.

"It's almost impossible to get hurt on this soft surface," Lucy said. "I'm going to throw you on your back while you try to stop me. Then we'll have a slow-action replay so that you can see how it was done."

She sounded completely self-assured as she crouched slightly with arms out in typical wrestling pose. "Come at me as fast and hard as you like," she ordered.

When Jack looked concerned, she added: "Don't worry, you won't hurt me; I'm almost indestructible!"

He smiled at her confidence and ran towards her. That was his first mistake: he had barely touched her before the world turned upside down and he was flying through the air to land flat on his back, unhurt but winded.

Lucy looked at him with amusement. "It's wise not to run at your opponent until you have more experience," she said, reaching down to help him up. "Your momentum made it quite easy for me to stoop and flip you over my head. Approach more carefully and you won't have so far to fall."

"You're not going to find it easy this time," Jack promised, feeling annoyed with himself for falling into her trap.

"That's the spirit!" she declared as he came towards her.

He managed to get a firm grip on both her shoulders with the intention of forcing her over sideways but she had braced herself with her feet wide apart and refused to yield more than an inch or two. She then leant over to press her forehead into the left side of his neck, at the same time bringing her left hand down hard on the pit of his right elbow, forcing his arm to bend further and bring them closer together. Then, with an astonishing surge of strength, she twisted them both round and somehow got her right leg against the outside of his. Giving another powerful heave, she rolled his whole body over her hip.

A fraction of a second later, he found himself flat on his back again.

"Normally, of course, I'd have you in a painful arm lock by now," she said, looking down at him with a smile.

Jack looked back up at her. "I'm not doing too well, am I?" he said ruefully.

"At least you tried," she replied. "Now we'll try again more slowly while I explain each move. Put your hands on my shoulders as you did before but don't try to resist this time, just watch and listen."

It was not long before he was flat on his back for the third time but at least he now had some idea of how it was done.

"You have a go now; I'll make it fairly easy for you," Lucy said.

They stood facing with their hands on each other's shoulders and Jack slowly went through the sequence, soon having the delight of rolling her supple body over his hip and on to the ground.

She looked up at him approvingly before springing nimbly to her feet. "Try again, but this time I'll offer some resistance. Be as rough as you like!"

"Actually I don't like; you're much too valuable," Jack said as he squared up to her once again. "I'll be semi-rough!"

Lucy chuckled as they closed in.

......

Jack managed to throw her twice more, using his right hip for the second time followed by his left. It was only as he was just about to use his left again that Lucy took him completely by surprise; she reached down with her right hand and, cupping it around the top of his left calf, pulled his leg forward so hard that he toppled backwards. The only difference this time was that he pulled her down on top of him.

With her face about five inches above his, it was all he could do to refrain from embracing her, but he soon sobered up when, back in instructor mode, she said sternly: "You took so long deciding what to do that you left yourself wide open for that one. By rights, I should now have you in a submission hold."

As she sprang up, she relented somewhat: "Never mind, you're beginning to get the hang of things. You practice the leg pull on me. It's easier than the hip roll if your arm is free, but, with a heavy opponent, you need to have strong arms and shoulders to get away with it."

"She certainly has those!" Jack thought.

......

When Lucy was satisfied that Jack had mastered this second version of the throw fairly well, she gave him a surprisingly cheeky smile.

"Before we take the mat back to the studio and relax over a bedtime drink, let's just go on wrestling until one of us gets a hold that the other can't break," she challenged.

"You're on," Jack replied in the same light-hearted vein, "but I only have a vague idea about submission holds from seeing the occasional TV program."

"It doesn't matter; it's just a bit of fun," she said as she faced him again.

Struggling against this amazing girl, he tried everything she had taught him but found her adept at foiling every move. On the other hand, she did not seem to be trying all that hard to throw him but was just enjoying the tussle.

At last, however, he managed to get her down. It was an untidy throw and he found himself on the mat in a potentially vulnerable position. Both Lucy's legs were free and she instantly used them to good effect by clamping his waist in a scissor grip.

Realising the danger of this position, Jack managed to twist himself round so that her thighs were now pressing on his back and stomach respectively, not on his more vulnerable sides. Even so he had to brace his stomach hard to resist the pressure she was exerting.

"Do you give up?" she asked, looking remarkably relaxed even though she sat twisted over at an uncomfortable angle propped up on one elbow.

Jack looked across at her, lying almost at right-angles to him. "Never!" he said firmly.

She said nothing but simply increased the power of her grip. He watched her superb thigh muscles harden even more. Not sure how much longer he could hold out, he began to wonder if punching the thigh in front of him might cause her grip to weaken.

Lucy saw his gaze and guessed what he might be thinking. "You're welcome to try punching me but I'm very tough!"

Jack grinned at her. "As I said earlier, I wouldn't dream of hurting you, but I must try something."

With that, he gripped the leg in front of him just above the knee and reached rather awkwardly behind him to do the same with her other leg. Twisting round as far as possible, he took a deep breath and attempted to prise her legs apart. Her strength was awesome and the pressure on his body only slackened slightly. However, he persevered and it eventually had some effect because Lucy spoke again.

"Although I could keep this up a lot longer, I suggest we call a truce because your hands are getting sweaty. If one of them slips, I might get a dislocated kneecap."

Jack nodded with some relief and they released each other.

Then to his astonishment, she seemed to see the funny side of things and tried to explain between chuckles: "I'm just imagining...what anybody peering over the fence might think...seeing two adults...who ought to know better...scrapping together like a couple of kids!"

Her mirth was contagious and it was not long before he was laughing too. They were still chuckling when they put the mat safely back in the studio.

"It's good to laugh sometimes; all the exercise over the last few days has been quite intense. Perhaps I've been too strict," she confessed as they walked back to the house.

"Not at all; I've needed every bit of it to get me going in earnest," Jack responded and really meant it. However, it was not until he taken their hot drinks to the sitting room that he had worked out what he wanted to get off his chest.

"I'm so glad I suggested our short visits to the pub at the beginning of our time here and you came up with the bright idea of the arm-wrestling sessions afterwards. It has helped to turn us into friends as well as partners for the difficult task ahead. For my part, I trust you completely now."

Lucy regarded him for a moment; then her face broke into a smile.

"It's the same for me," she said. "In fact, I would go so far as to say that I would trust you with my life, although I hope it won't have to come to that!"

"Russian mafia and alpine landslides permitting!" said Jack, feeling so pleased with her response that he raised his right hand in a high-five salutation.

Without hesitation, she met his open hand with hers but not with the usual slap; instead, she let her hand rest against his for a moment. The gesture seemed to be her way of signifying that they were now comrades in arms, but, sadly, he could detect no sign that she thought of him as a potential boyfriend.

Chapter 5: The Five Sisters of Kintail

The Highlands greeted Jack and Lucy with heavy rain soon after the camper van had skirted Loch Lomond.

Jack drove most of the way because he was the more experienced driver, having once owned an elderly Ford Fiesta before it failed its MOT and been too expensive to repair. After a second coffee break in Crianlarich, just north of the Trossachs National Park, Lucy gave him a break by taking over the wheel as far as Fort William.

Here they had a meal in the café attached to the Morrison's supermarket next to the bus and train stations and Lucy took the opportunity to study the road map John had lent them.

"Unfortunately, we have to go quite a long way northeast towards Inverness on the A82 before we can turn west at Invergarry and take the A87 for the final 36 miles to the caravan park in Morvich," she said.

"At least we'll see part of the famous Great Glen that goes all the way from Fort William to Inverness, especially now that the rain is easing off," Jack replied, trying to look on the bright side.

......

The A87 turned out to be a pleasant road that threaded its way through the mountains. A few miles before reaching their destination, Lucy noticed a high ridge on the right-hand side of the road that appeared to be formed of a chain of closely spaced mountains.

Jack was delighted to be able to answer her query. "Those mountains are called the Five Sisters of Kintail and there's a challenging eight-hour hike along the ridge that should be ideal for trail-running. I downloaded a map from the Walk Highlands website before we came away. The northern end of the ridge can be accessed from the hamlet of Allt a Chruinn, where we'll be turning off to get to Morvich, and the southern end from a small lay-by that we must have passed a minute or two ago. I also discovered that three of the Sisters are classed as Munros, which means that they're over 3000 ft in height: that's about 914m. Munro is the name of the man who first climbed and classified all such mountains in Scotland, although I believe he missed one or two."

"I think you've done a brilliant job with all this research," Lucy said. "I'm pretty useless with computers!"

"Well, you're pretty good at a lot of other things!" Jack answered firmly.

Lucy failed to react to this compliment and continued to think of their future plans. "It's now Wednesday and we're returning to Terregles first thing on Sunday. That gives us three whole days to fit in as much running as possible," she said, re-iterating what they already knew. "So, if the weather permits, I suggest two tough warm-up days before we really test ourselves running that trail non-stop in both directions. If we save time by not descending all the way to the main road at the southern end, we should be able to complete it in less than ten hours."

"That's a challenge to look forward to!" Jack exclaimed. "If we do that successfully then we can certainly tackle whatever Switzerland throws at us!"

......

Finally, after a tortuous 245-mile journey, Jack thankfully turned right off the A87 at Allt a Chruinn at the head of Loch Duich and drove a final mile or so inland to the caravan site in Morvich.

They parked the camper van in the space allocated to them and Jack connected up the electricity. On his brief visit to Terregles the previous afternoon, John had informed them that the van's water tank would have to be topped up manually but that there was an excellent shower and toilet block with plenty of hot water.

39

It was now late afternoon, and, feeling the need to stretch their legs, the young couple walked back as far as the main road for a proper look at Loch Duich. They stood on the waterside pavement and gazed down the long stretch of water. The rain had ceased completely and there was even a small patch of blue sky.

"This is a sea loch and eventually joins Loch Alsh before reaching the open sea near Kyle of Lochalsh where there's a bridge over to the island of Skye," Jack said. "One day I'll bring a bicycle by train to Fort William and explore this whole area on two wheels."

"It certainly is a lovely spot and the surrounding mountains and glens look very promising for some serious running," Lucy said. "Thank you for all the driving you've done to get us here."

She looked across at Jack with a smile. But he was even more surprised when, on sudden impulse, she slipped her arm through his.

......

They had only walked a short distance back down the lane towards the caravan park when Jack pointed to a service road on the right that curved out of sight behind a small dwelling.

"That leads to the Five Sisters trail," he said. "I looked at this entrance on Google Maps so that we would know where to find it."

With a sense of anticipation, they returned to the caravan park and Lucy prepared supper from the stock of food Mrs McCready had provided.

"Before today, I only experienced your boiled eggs at breakfast but now I can congratulate you on your cooking skills," Jack said as they ate the meal at a small folding table he had set up just outside the van.

They were both so weary after the long journey that they decided to delay having a shower until early the following morning. The bunk beds in the van looked small and uncomfortable, but, as it turned out, they were both surprised at how quickly and peacefully the night passed.

......

The advantage of using the shower block early was that it was almost empty and so it was not long before Lucy was preparing bacon and eggs for breakfast.

After a suitable interval to let their food settle, the two young people were more than ready to test themselves on some serious gradients. They decided to start with a 6-mile run up to the Falls of Glomach: one of the possible treks Jack had researched on Google Maps.

"The path is actually part of the Scottish National Trail that continues all the way to Cape Wrath on the northwest tip of Scotland," he informed Lucy. "It starts out as a gentle climb but gets very steep before reaching about 500m and then dropping down again to 300m at the top of the Falls. After a sightseeing stop, we can either continue down a steep path into Glen Elchaig that the Walk Highlands website warns can be slippery in bad weather, or do some fell-running on the slopes above the Falls."

"I suggest the latter, especially after yesterday's heavy rain," Lucy said. "We could even have a race up a couple of mountains and eat our sandwiches on top of one of them!"

Jack offered to carry all the water in his rucksack but Lucy insisted that they share the load as evenly as possible before they walked to the entrance of the caravan park and turned left down the narrow lane leading away from Morvich and east into the mountains.

"I'll lead; see if you can keep up with me!" she said, giving him one of the friendly but challenging looks he had come to know so well. With that parting shot, she set off at a jog that quickly turned into smooth running motion.

41

"There's no way I'm going to let Supergirl leave me behind," Jack promised himself as he followed close on her heels.

The initial part of the journey was fairly level but Lucy maintained almost the same steady pace as the gradient increased. She only slowed to a jog when the path became really steep.

After only one short stop for a few sips of water, the young couple finally crested the peak of the ridge and dropped gradually down into a long shallow valley. The noise of cascading water increased but it was still out of sight when they reached a notice-board that stated: "Falls of Glomach. Danger – Please take great care".

Rather surprisingly, three hikers were having a picnic on the grass.

"Wow; you look as if you've run all the way up here!" a middle-aged man said.

"We have, almost non-stop," Lucy replied. "We're camping down in Morvich."

"So are we," one of the two women said. "We were awake so early that we thought we'd bring our breakfast up here on such a nice morning. Do have a cup of coffee with us before you climb down to see the Falls; they're really spectacular and have a drop of over 100m."

"That's very kind of you; we've only got water," Jack said gratefully, producing two picnic mugs from his rucksack. "Running is thirsty work!" he added as an afterthought.

The kind woman produced a large thermos flask and shared the remains of the coffee between the two mugs. "It's getting tepid but tastes OK," she said.

"At least I've now got an empty flask to carry back; it weighed a ton by the time I got up here," the man remarked as he began to pack the remains of the picnic into three rucksacks.

"We left at six-thirty and took well over two and a half hours to get up here. How long did it take you two fit young people?" the second woman asked.

"About 70 minutes," Jack said. "We're trying our hand at fell-running for the first time."

"We're planning to run up some of the slopes around here," Lucy volunteered. "But thank you for the coffee; it made a nice change from water."

They parted company with friendly waves and began the careful descent to see the Falls at close quarters.

"This view alone makes it worth coming all the way up here!" Jack exclaimed as he produced a small digital camera from his rucksack. Lucy could only nod in agreement; she was completely fascinated by the impressive sight.

They climbed back up to the top and began walking beside the narrow river feeding the Falls. It was pleasant to watch the water bubble its way past small rocks as it meandered through a glen flanked by grass-covered slopes that looked remarkably friendly in the bright sunshine.

"None of these peaks is more than about 500m and so we'll be running or scrambling up about 200m from here. You choose first," Jack said.

"What about that one?" Lucy said, pointing.

"OK, but it means finding some stepping stones or taking our trainers off and wading."

They eventually managed to find a spot where it was possible to step from one stone to another without getting too wet.

Having selected a prominent rock on the mountain top to aim for, Lucy said: "Now for a flat-out race by any route you care to take. Are you ready? Get set. Go!"

They pounded up the slope along closely parallel routes, trying to avoid large rocks and areas of very rough ground. As they neared the top, it became obvious that Lucy was marginally ahead. Jack did everything he could to speed up, but it was to no avail and she beat him by about ten feet.

They were so out of breath that they had to lean on each other for support. Finally, Jack gasped: "Well done; you were fantastic."

"You were pretty good yourself. You'll have a chance to get even with your choice of slope," Lucy said as they began the descent.

......

Jack was secretly delighted when he managed to outrun her to the outcrop of rock he selected. They were surprised to find, however, that the highest point of the mountain was a short distance away.

"Let's scramble up there and have our sandwiches. The views should be good on a day like this," Lucy suggested.

She was right and they had an enjoyable lunch break perched on a couple of small rocks surrounded by the splendidly mountainous landscape.

......

That evening, the radio in the camper van provided the welcome news that the fine weather would last for another two days, give or take the occasional shower. Lucy and Jack therefore decided to run southwest down the Scottish National Trail to Cluanie Inn on the A87 the next day and leave the final challenge of a non-stop run along the Five Sisters ridge until Saturday. After a refreshment break at the Inn, they would run back, making a total distance of about 34 miles.

"I know the Cluanie trip is longer than the Five Sisters one but we'll only be climbing to a mere 400m fairly slowly before dropping down to Loch Cluanie at 200m," Jack said. "We'll also be able to have a decent break if we leave fairly early in the morning."

"So it's early to bed again," Lucy commented.

......

At 8:05 the next morning, they left the caravan park in the same direction as on the previous day and very soon reached a signpost pointing down a track on the right-hand side of the lane that read: "To Cluanie via Glen Lichd"

"This is where the National Trail comes into Morvich from the south," Jack informed Lucy. "We go through this pedestrian gate and follow the rough vehicle track along the southern side of the River Croe. Watch out for the sheep!"

He led the way for most of the morning with Lucy quite content to follow at his preferred pace. The scenery was quite spectacular and the only time they had to slow down significantly was over some boggy ground.

Eventually, they dropped down into Glen Cluanie with the water on Loch Cluanie sparkling in the sunlight.

"We have to turn right here," Jack said when they arrived on the A87. "The Inn should be less than half a mile. I'm hungry!"

Lucy laughed. "That makes two of us. Anyway that was excellent exercise; by the time we leave Scotland we'll have legs of steel."

"Yours already are as far as I'm concerned," Jack responded.

She laughed and linked arms with him as they walked towards the isolated white building that had come into sight. It was just after midday; there would be plenty of time for a nourishing main course and leisurely cold drink before returning to Morvich.

......

Very early on Saturday morning, Lucy prepared a modest breakfast while Jack made up some sandwiches and filled their water bottles. All this activity was a tight squeeze in the small van but he was pleased to have the excuse to be close to the girl he loved.

They had earlier agreed that Lucy would lead on the outbound journey over the Five Sister's trail and that Jack

45

would bring them back after a short refreshment break at some suitable spot high above the A87.

They were ready to leave by 7:10. As Lucy shouldered her rucksack, she remarked: "I feel fitter than ever after all our training over the last two and a half weeks. I can see it's done you good as well."

She looked at him with a smile that warmed his heart. Nevertheless, she was still an enigma to him; although invariably friendly, she seemed to be holding herself back.

......

There was hardly any traffic and so they ran side-by-side back towards Allt a Chruinn until turning left into the narrow service road Jack had pointed out three days earlier. Lucy grinned at him and drew ahead to take the lead position.

They were soon on a track that ran up beside the stream giving the hamlet its name. It eventually narrowed to become a rough stony path and it was now clear that they were heading for the north-western flank of a low mountain named Beinn Bhuidhe.

The path petered out for a time and Lucy was forced to slow down to avoid some boggy ground before they passed a waterfall and left the stream to begin the really serious climb up the flank of the mountain.

Not for the first time, Jack delighted in following his athletic companion as she powered her way up, seemingly almost oblivious to the effort needed. It was not until the path took them a short distance below the summit of Beinn Bhuidhe that she stopped for a drink of water.

Breathing deeply, her eyes were shining with pleasure. "That's what I call a good test of endurance; it must have been at least 500m!"

Jack looked at her and smiled as he tried to get his breath back. Only she could have led him up so quickly; he really was hopelessly in love with this incredible girl. He took her hand under the pretext of encouraging her to look back the way they had come.

A superb panorama stretched out below them: the whole of Loch Duich was backed by mountains that disappeared into the distant haze.

"Those are almost certainly the mountains of Skye in the far distance," he said as he got his small camera out. "What a view!" But he could not help thinking that the best view of all was that of the girl beside him.

"This is splendid but let's get going again," she said enthusiastically.

And so they ran on at a good pace but taking great care of their footing; the path, such as it was, wound precariously between rocks and coarse grass and often crossed large areas of solid rock.

The route continued to take them over or close to mountain summits before dropping down into deep cols or following the top of narrow ridges. It was rather like trying to traverse an enormous switchback. In fact, it was often easier to run up the inclines to the next peak before descending more cautiously.

......

Lucy and Jack had an almost triumphant water stop beside the cairn on the summit of the highest Munro of the Five Sisters – Sgurr Fhuaran – where they felt as if they were on top of the world, almost literally.

When Jack had managed to control his breathing, he said: "Sgurr means "peak" in Gaelic and Fhuaran means "fountain" but it's hard to see why this should be called Fountain Peak."

"Anyway, the views are spectacular even if a little misty," Lucy said.

......

After three more mountain peaks – two of them Munros – Jack was thankful and all too ready for something to eat when Lucy finally decided that the path was beginning to drop down sharply towards the main road that wound ribbon-like through Glen Shiel well over 500m below them.

"Lunchtime I think, if we can find somewhere that's not too damp to sit down," she said.

She did not allow much time for their modest repast, however, and soon stood up to say: "It's your turn to lead us back. We've made good time so far and should be able to get back by five o'clock if you keep up the pressure."

"OK boss!" Jack said, grinning at his energetic companion.

Their first water stop on the return journey was close to the summit of Sgurr nan Spainteach.

"I read that this name means Peak of the Spaniards," Jack informed his companion. "It was named in honour of 300 Spanish soldiers who fought alongside the defeated Jacobite rebels in the Battle of Glen Shiel in 1719."

"You really are a mine of information!" Lucy said admiringly.

It was not long, however, before the afternoon became a real slog as far as Jack was concerned, but he dug deep and kept going and, at long last, was leading the way down the flank of Beinn Bhuidhe with their destination in sight.

All the way along the ridge, Lucy had deliberately positioned herself sufficiently far back to avoid putting him under pressure. He was grateful for her consideration but could sense that even she would be glad to be home.

......

The first thing the young couple did on reaching the camper van was to have a long drink of water. Then it was off to the shower block to refresh their weary bodies and get cleaned up.

"I don't think I've ever sweated so much," Jack said as they entered.

"Never mind," Lucy said. "If we leave really early tomorrow, we should get back in time to put our dirty washing in the machine and get it dry by the following day."

It was while they were consuming two mugs of tea and the last of the fruit cake at the table outside the van that Jack plucked up courage to offer an invitation.

"May I invite you to come with me to Kintail Lodge Hotel for dinner tonight as a thank-you for all your training? Without you, I would never have achieved what I have. You've been really brilliant!"

Lucy looked at him, surprised and strangely pleased. "Thank you, I'd love to come. I'm still ravenous after that slice of cake and there's not much food left."

Jack's heart missed a beat. "Good! I'll book a table for seven-thirty. It's about two miles away but we can walk normally for a change!"

Lucy laughed. "There's even time for a short lie down," she said as she picked up their empty mugs and took them inside the van.

Jack soon followed her; a rest did indeed sound attractive even on such a small bunk.

Chapter 6: The Dinner Date

Lucy looked across the table at Jack while they sipped their drinks and waited for the food he had ordered. Thoughts crowded her mind.

"I'm almost twenty and this is the first man I've ever enjoyed having as a friend. I've been so focussed on proving that a woman can be just as strong and fit as a man that I've come to regard them as the opposition. It's not been much better with girls of my own age and I've no close friends. Maybe there's something wrong with me, unless it's just my poor start in life. Jack has such a kind face. Perhaps I should tell him about it."

Jack, for his part, gazed back at Lucy with a happy smile. He was relieved that he had acquitted himself well on the run. Although he had no inkling of the thoughts flooding through her head, he sensed she was troubled in some way and felt a quite extraordinary sympathy and tenderness for her.

The main course arrived and they ate hungrily, exchanging brief smiles of appreciation and the occasional comment. It was not until starting on the apple pie and ice-cream that Lucy finally decided to take the plunge.

"May I tell you why I got into fitness in a big way? You'll be the first person I've ever told." She looked uncharacteristically nervous.

"Of course you may! I'd love to hear about it; anything you say will remain with me," Jack replied gently.

Lucy smiled with relief; an invisible barrier was about to be breached.

"It all started after my parents were killed in a car accident when I was ten years old," she said slowly. "Placed in a foster home, I was inconsolable for weeks. My foster parents were kind and understanding and things eventually improved, but, quite frankly, I still felt miserable and was a completely messed up kid: overweight, inattentive at school and hopeless at games. It all came to a head one day during a mixed game of basketball. The ball was passed to me at a crucial stage and I dropped it, allowing the opposition to score vital points. One of the boys in my team stormed up to me afterwards. "Why don't you just give up, you complete weed!" he shouted threateningly.

"Not surprisingly, I burst into tears, which only made matters worse. When my foster-father came home from work, he could see that something was wrong and persuaded me to tell him, whereupon he took me by the hand and led me down the garden to his prize vegetable plot. He pointed to a miserable-looking weed that was barely surviving in the shade of a large cabbage leaf and then to another far more robust specimen in a sunny spot. "Those are exactly the same type of weed but only one of them is flourishing," he commented.

"Then he added something I'll never forget. "Weeds have no control over where and how they grow. On the other hand, God has given human beings freewill and therefore the possibility of choice. While you're young you must live with the adults who look after you but you can still exercise some control over how you live. My advice to you is to move out from the dark place you're in at the moment and walk into the light, taking hold of some of the opportunities available to youngsters these days."

"Well, that proved to be the catalyst I needed. I started taking lots of exercise, worked hard at school and, not least, lost weight! I was greatly helped by a magazine on health and fitness that I now suspect had been carefully left out for me to find; it showed slim attractive women doing all sorts of aerobic exercises. Of course, I started in a low key way but gradually got more and more ambitious and involved in athletic pursuits. I've continued to do so ever since."

She stopped suddenly, embarrassed at having revealed so much for the first time in her life. She blushed and looked down to concentrate on the last spoonful of apple pie.

51

"Thank you for sharing something so personal. With such an unhappy start, you've been remarkably successful in "walking into the light". Your foster father is a wise man," Jack said softly.

Lucy nodded, now too moved to say anything further. Her eyes were full of tears.

Jack realized she would feel more comfortable if they left the crowded restaurant and so he quickly paid the bill.

......

They walked slowly down the loch-side path as it skirted a small wood on its way back to the main road.

"Thank you for a splendid meal," Lucy said. "I'm sorry to have spoiled it by talking so much and shedding a few tears."

"You were recalling the terrible experience of a young child faced with the sudden loss of parents, followed by being made to feel useless and rejected," Jack replied. "I'm very privileged to have been allowed to share them. Tears help to sooth the pain."

His words and the gentleness in his voice seemed to open a floodgate; Lucy began to sob quietly. He put his arm around her shoulders and led her away from the path to the water's edge.

"Let the tears come," he whispered. "You've bottled everything up far too long. Perhaps you've never allowed yourself as an adult to grieve for losing the parents you loved."

He continued to hold her tight. His tenderness was almost palpable, so much so that Lucy seemed to draw comfort and strength from him and gradually recovered until she became completely still with her head resting against his shoulder.

"Thank you for being so kind and understanding," she whispered eventually and pulled away so that she could link arms with him, ready to head back to the campsite.

He squeezed the firmly muscled arm threaded through his. "I'll always be there for you. After our task in Switzerland

52

is finished, perhaps we could keep in touch; Lancaster and Leeds are not all that far apart!"

Lucy looked at him, her eyes still red with crying. Then, totally out of character, she smiled impishly.

"What would you say to the idea of regarding the coming week in Switzerland as our first date? I promise to leave my training hat behind in Terregles so that we can get to know each other properly."

Jack was so stunned and delighted by her suggestion that it took him a second or two to reply.

"There's nothing I'd like better; you're the most amazing girl I've ever met," he whispered and very gently swung her round to hug her. He made no attempt to kiss her because he sensed that she was still feeling exposed and vulnerable after taking him into her confidence.

As they made their way back along the dark lane to the campsite, he said very quietly: "We've got plenty of time and can take things slowly; after all we'll be in each other's company almost continuously!"

He could sense Lucy relaxing even further.

"We're certainly going to find it quite easy to act as John's happy couple!" she said, laughing for the first time that evening.

Back in the camper van, they were now so weary after the strenuous day that they slipped into a deep sleep almost as soon as their heads touched the pillows.

Chapter 7: The Bodleian Library

By two o'clock on Monday afternoon, John, Lucy and Jack were seated at a quiet table near the back of a café not far from Carlisle station. The young couple would soon be leaving on the four-hour train journey to Oxford via Wolverhampton where John had booked a twin-bedded room for two nights in the YHA hostel almost next door to Oxford station.

He handed over a rough sketch map of the centre of Oxford together with their train tickets, a receipt for the hostel and an envelope addressed to the Director of the Bodleian Library.

"You'll have time tonight to reconnoitre the centre of Oxford and the outside of the Old Bodleian Library on the corner of Broad Street and Catte Street," he said. "The Great Gate entrance is on Catte Street. On Tuesday morning, take your passports as proof of identity, buy tickets at the office inside the gate just like the other visitors and make your way casually to the information desk on the first floor beside the north staircase. Aim to be there at 10:45 and give this letter to the person on duty; then wait to be discretely taken to a private office.

"The manuscript will be in a protective waterproof wrapping but disguised in some way to make it look like something bought from the museum shop. I suggest you walk around the building for a short time like normal visitors before you leave. After that keep the manuscript in a small rucksack or similar and carry it with you at all times."

Then John handed Jack a thick envelope. "This contains £200 for your expenses in the UK, a ticket for the early morning express coach from Oxford to Heathrow Terminal 5, your airline tickets, return rail tickets from Basle to Interlaken, and 2,000 Swiss francs – mainly in 100 CHF notes to reduce bulk. There's also a note giving the name and location of the café in Kandersteg and the date and time you must be there.

Finally, after your return to Heathrow, you'll need to buy London Transport tickets to get you to Euston station but I've enclosed the train tickets from Euston to Carlisle, where I've booked you a room at the Hotel Ibis and warned them that you won't be there until soon after 10 pm on Thursday week. Have a lie in on the Friday morning and come to see me for a debriefing at eleven o'clock. I may even take you out for a celebration lunch!

"You should have plenty of cash but if you need to make any emergency payments by credit or debit card, keep the receipts and you'll be reimbursed. By the way, for extra security, I've made all these arrangements from home and not from the office. You may have noticed that I made an excuse to get Amy out of the room for part of the time on the interview day. It's not that I don't trust her but simply that the fewer people who know all the details, the better. I've no idea how much this unique Russian manuscript might raise at auction but it would be very substantial; so guard it well and don't let the mafia get their hands on it!"

He looked at them and smiled. "I think that's all, except to wish you a safe journey and successful mission."

He stood up ready to shake hands but then something suddenly occurred to him and he sat down again. "I nearly forgot; I haven't given you my mobile 'phone number. Don't use it before the manuscript is delivered unless there's an emergency."

He felt in his pocket for a piece of paper and then noticed a blank card, about the size of a business card, lying on the table.

"I'll use this," he said and wrote his number on the card before giving it to Jack who tucked it safely in his wallet. "Now I really will leave you to finish your sandwich and drink. Don't miss your train!"

......

Lucy looked out of the window of their modest but clean room in the YHA hostel. "At least we're not overlooking the railway," she said thankfully.

Jack was relieved, not so much at the thought of a reasonably peaceful night but because Lucy had been rather glum ever since John had left them in the Carlisle café. It was only towards the end of the long train journey that he had guessed the probable cause; John had entrusted him with the envelope containing all their tickets and not her.

"I'm an idiot," he thought. "It would have been politic to give it to her to put in her shoulder bag. Perhaps this room has helped to cheer her up, especially as it has a nice shower."

He opened the precious envelope and spread everything out on his bed in logical order. The Swiss banknotes all seemed to be new ones.

"I hope these are not forgeries!" he said with a chuckle as he divided the amount equally. "I suggest we each take half for safety."

"No; you have a money-belt and so it would be sensible for you to take all the 100 franc notes; just give me a few of the lower denominations," Lucy said firmly. "You can reduce the amount you're carrying by paying for the nights in Wilderswil as soon as we arrive."

......

Not long after seven o'clock, the young couple walked towards the centre of Oxford on the lookout for somewhere to eat. More by luck than design, they passed an Italian restaurant near Oxford Castle and had a pleasant meal at a table on the outside terrace.

During the meal, Lucy looked at Jack apologetically. "I'm sorry for my grumpiness during the journey from Carlisle; very stupidly I allowed myself to be miffed when John automatically assumed you should be in charge of all the paperwork."

"I only realized that might be the problem just before we reached Oxford," he replied. "For my part, I've always assumed we're equal partners. I couldn't have a better one than you!"

She gave him a beaming smile. "So I'm forgiven and we're still good friends?"

"Of course, and always will be," came the positive reply.

......

They left the restaurant and continued to walk east until reaching the High Street. Not far past Brasenose College they stopped to ask the way to the Bodleian Library and were directed north up a pedestrian passage into Catte Street.

"That's good; John's sketch map shows the northern end of Catte Street and so we just follow our noses," Jack said thankfully.

They passed the circular Radcliffe Camera and came to the Old Library and its Great Gate, now securely closed by a massive oak-panelled door.

"So this is where we come tomorrow morning," he remarked.

Arriving at the junction with Broad Street, he guided Lucy left past the Sheldonian Theatre, also circular and even more impressive than the Radcliffe Camera. They crossed the wide street and paused to look in the windows of Blackwell's enormous bookshop.

"I think it's time to head back," Jack said. "I can use John's sketch map now; we just need to continue west along here."

"Perhaps we could stop for a hot drink on the way," Lucy said, unexpectedly linking arms with her companion.

He looked down at her with a happy smile.

......

The Bodleian Library had only recently opened and was not busy when Lucy and Jack made their way to the information desk. The whole transaction went smoothly.

Within ten minutes, the young couple were mingling with other visitors walking around the impressive building, at the same time surreptitiously keeping a wary eye out for anyone who might be taking an interest in them. Unfortunately, Jack had to hold the parcel discretely under his arm because it was too large for Lucy's small shoulder bag.

"I need some good sun cream; let's find the main shopping area," Lucy said. "I also suggest having our main meal at lunchtime. Not only was the breakfast disappointing but we need a really early night because we have to be up at five o'clock to get to the coach station on time!"

The rest of the day passed happily. They explored more of the city centre and had a pleasant walk along the bank of the Thames, or Isis as it is called in Oxford. By the time they were making their way back to the hostel, they were getting on so well that Jack had high hopes for what might transpire between them in Switzerland.

Chapter 8: The Jungfrau

Rain lashed the windows of Intercity Express IC61 from Basle to Interlaken as the long train reached its first stop at Olten. In fact, not only did it have twelve coaches but they were double-decker and the young couple had the novelty of sitting on the top deck of a train for the first time.

"Would you like a cup of coffee?"Jack asked, prompted by the fact that they had stopped opposite the station buffet.

"Yes please, provided you don't have to get off the train. I'd hate to go on without you, especially as you have our tickets!" Lucy replied.

"There's a buffet car about two carriages away; it's called a Restaurant Bistro," he said as he disappeared.

Ten minutes later, he returned with two coffees. "I'm most impressed; there's a much better selection than in the UK and about half the lower deck of one carriage is given over to tables," he reported. "If you'd like anything else we can go along and sit in comfort; we didn't have much to eat at Heathrow."

A little later, they decided to investigate together and, soon after leaving Berne, Jack impressed Lucy by using what sounded like fluent German to ask the couple in the seat opposite to keep an eye on their luggage.

Taking his shoulder bag with the precious manuscript and all their documents, he led her back down the train to have an excellent bowl of soup with fresh bread while they watched the attractive countryside speed past.

"This is the first time I've ever had anything to eat in a dining car," Lucy said. "I'm really enjoying myself."

"I'm so glad," Jack responded. "The scenery is about to get even better because the mountains are just coming into sight. For the last part of the journey, we'll have mountains on our right and Lake Thun on our left."

They had barely finished the soup before the train reached the town of Thun. "Now the views really begin," he promised. "It's a pity there's no sun."

It was still raining, although not nearly so hard as earlier, but the novelty of her surroundings was such that Lucy did not mind.

The train stopped again soon after they had returned to their seats. Looking out at the platform signboard, Jack saw that it was Spiez.

"When we transfer to Adelboden next Sunday, we'll be coming back here to get a train to a place called Frutigen and, finally, a bus," he said.

Lucy looked at him in surprise. "How do you know all these details?"

"I looked them up on the Swiss Railways website," he replied, glad that she was impressed by his efficiency.

He produced a street map from his shoulder bag. "This is a map of Interlaken that I picked up on my last visit. There are two stations, Interlaken West and Ost. The railway serving the two valleys forming the Jungfrau region leaves from Interlaken Ost. The first stop is Wilderswil, about two miles to the south, and our guesthouse is three minutes walk from the station." He pointed to the places mentioned on the small map.

Lucy was intrigued to see that a river ran through the town joining Lake Thun to Lake Brienz and that there was a steamer terminal for the latter very close to Interlaken Ost.

"I wonder if we'll have time for a trip on the water," she thought hopefully.

"You'll see from the map that Interlaken West is slightly closer to Wilderswil as the crow flies and so you may prefer to walk after sitting for so long," Jack suggested.

"That's a good idea, especially as our cabin bags can be worn as backpacks," Lucy said. "It's also stopped raining, thank goodness."

......

"Of course, this is your second visit to Switzerland and Interlaken because you came to stay with your friend," Lucy commented as they threaded their way through the streets with the aid of Jack's map at about six-fifteen. Even though a lot of the shops had shut, the town was still surprisingly busy.

"Yes, it was a very pleasant week about two years ago and Nicolas took me to several breathtaking places that I'm looking forward to showing you," Jack acknowledged.

"His parents are lovely folk; the family name is Gerber but they'll want us to use their first names – Daniel and Lara. Nicolas tells me that his father has now retired; he used to be a mechanical engineer working somewhere in Interlaken. That may be why Nicolas followed in his footsteps and now has an excellent job in the States. We exchange emails fairly frequently.

"By the way, they only have two en-suite double bedrooms and one small single, which I had two years ago. When I sent an email giving the dates we wanted and our approximate time of arrival, Lara replied that their twin room was already taken but we could have their other room that has a bed consisting of a large wooden frame with two single mattresses and separate duvets; this is an arrangement often found in Austria and Switzerland. She obviously assumes that we're a couple; otherwise, why would we be going on a walking holiday together? Anyway, I promise to behave myself!"

"You'd better or you'll be sorry; this is only the first day of our "date"!" Lucy replied, but the smile she gave him softened the comment.

......

"Welcome, welcome, do come in!" Lara Geber said, opening the door of the small guesthouse and standing back with a beaming smile.

61

Lucy was astonished when the woman threw her arms around Jack and kissed him before turning to shake her hand vigorously.

"Lara, this is Lucy," Jack said. "Lucy, this is Nicolas' mother who thoroughly spoiled me when I stayed here two years ago."

"Nonsense, you fully deserved to be spoiled," Lara replied.

She looked at Lucy with a twinkle in her eye. "I don't suppose Jack has told you how he and Nicolas met in Sheffield three years ago, has he?"

Lucy shook her head. "No, do tell me," she said curiously, at the same time surprised by Lara's excellent command of English.

"Well, late one evening Nicolas was walking back to his lodgings when two teenage thugs tried to mug him; one of them even pointed a knife at his throat! Apparently Jack appeared from nowhere and fought them off, punching one to the ground before they both ran away. Nicolas and Jack then became firm friends; my husband and I can testify to how much that helped our son settle down and enjoy his nine months at Sheffield University."

"I'm only glad I happened to be there at the right moment," Jack said, feeling rather embarrassed.

Lucy, however, had an enigmatic expression on her face. "Quite a hero in fact!" she said.

"He's certainly that," Lara murmured before saying more loudly: "Let me show you to your room. As soon as you're ready, come down to the breakfast room and have a hot drink; there's a jug of coffee on the hot plate. You must be tired, thirsty and hungry after your long journey. Daniel and I would be honoured if you would eat with us tonight. You have three more evenings to try out restaurants in the area, so please say yes!"

"Thank you, we'd love to have a meal with you; it's very kind of you to invite us," Lucy said, after a quick glance at Jack.

"Splendid! Daniel will be home soon, so shall we say eight o'clock? I'm preparing a special braised beef dish," Lara said as she showed them upstairs to a nice airy room that overlooked a small back garden mainly given over to growing vegetables and herbs.

Lucy was relieved when she saw that Jack had been right; the double bed did indeed consist of two mattresses in a large frame and separate duvets. Jack politely let her choose her preferred side and she slipped her pyjamas under the pillow to stake her claim before they returned downstairs for a welcome cup of coffee.

......

Daniel Geber was almost as delighted as his wife to meet Jack again when the young couple came down to the Geber's basement apartment a couple of minutes after eight o'clock.

The meal started with a delicious homemade vegetable soup. "This is amazing soup! Are the vegetables from your garden?" Lucy asked.

"Some of them are but the taste is all down to my wife's skill," Daniel replied proudly. "But do tell us why you've come to Switzerland. Lara and I wondered if you might be on honeymoon but I can't see a wedding ring!"

Lucy blushed and Jack hurried to put things straight.

"No!" he laughed. "We're just very good friends and love trail running. In fact, we've done some running in the Scottish Highlands but the highest we've been so far is about half the height of Kleine Scheidegg where we hope to go tomorrow when we cross over from Grindelwald to Lauterbrunnen. Then we'll either run back here or get the train, depending on how we feel."

"If we run the whole way, Jack has estimated it to be nearly 20 miles, or 30km. I know that doesn't sound very far

63

but we'll be climbing over 1000m and coming down even further, and, of course, we're not yet accustomed to these heights," Lucy added.

Daniel looked surprised. "You must be very fit," he said admiringly.

Jack looked at Lucy with a proud smile. "Lucy certainly is and she keeps me on my toes!"

Meanwhile Lara had cleared the soup dishes and brought in the main course, "This is a speciality from the Italian part of Switzerland: polenta and braised beef," she said. "I hope you like it; polenta is a porridge made of maize."

"It smells delicious!" Lucy said.

......

"That was a splendid meal last night. Mr and Mrs Geber are such nice people," Lucy said as they sat on the train to Grindelwald the following morning.

"It was and they are," Jack agreed, rather absentmindedly. He was looking at a local walking map purchased on the way to Wilderswil station to refresh his memory.

The weather looked promising with intermittent sunshine and so they were aiming to do the run Jack had outlined the previous evening. The first and toughest leg would be the six mile climb from Grindelwald at just over 1000m to Kleine Scheidegg, the top of the pass, at 2060m.

The train came to a stop at a small station and there was the sound of activity on the platform.

"The train divides here," Jack told his companion. "The front four carriages carry on south to Lauterbrunnen in one valley and our half takes the longer route east to Grindelwald in the next valley."

......

The train climbed slowly into Grindelwald Dorf station and the young couple alighted, almost overwhelmed by the sight of the surrounding mountains at close quarters even when veiled in cloud.

As they left the station and began to walk up the main street, Jack pointed across the road to a narrow path that disappeared out of sight down a steep slope. A tall post at the entrance carried a cluster of direction signs.

"I think that's the way we need to go after a quick look round the village. Fortunately, all the walks are well signposted," he said. "There's a narrow-gauge railway that goes up to Kleine Scheidegg and our path will come quite close to it from time to time. The famous Jungfraujoch cog-railway takes over at Kleine Scheidegg and climbs to a height of nearly 3,500m; Jungfraujoch is the name of the saddle between the Mönch and the Jungfrau. It's an expensive trip but very popular with tourists.

"The first part of our route to Kleine Scheidegg will be on what's known as the Eiger Ultra Trail, at least as far as Alpiglen station where the Trail loops back towards Grindelwald. From Alpiglen, we just continue to follow the signs to Kleine Scheidegg," he concluded.

"I'm really looking forward to seeing the Eiger, Mönch and Jungfrau properly if these clouds lift," Lucy said. "I saw a postcard of all three mountains together when we passed a shop on the way to the Wilderswil station; they looked amazing even in miniature!"

Jack had never heard her sound so enthusiastic. "In the meantime, look over there to the east; that's the Wetterhorn," he said.

She followed his pointing hand. A hole had been rapidly forming in the clouds as they walked and now the top of a solitary snow-capped mountain rose majestically into the clear blue oval patch of sky. Surrounded by a frame of clouds, it was as if she was staring at an exquisite cameo.

"Oh, how splendid!" Lucy whispered as she grabbed Jack's hand in her desire to share this moment of awe.

"Perhaps that's a foretaste of things to come," he said happily.

Their hands remained linked as they headed back towards the station and the start of their challenging run.

......

Jack set a brisk pace down to one of the bridges crossing the turbulent river below the village centre and then began the long climb. At first, the small signs to Kleine Scheidegg directed them up paved roads that gradually became narrower, but then he spotted a sign on the right-hand side of the road pointing up a flight of steps. Here he sensibly slowed down, even when the steps reverted to a steep path. They were both glad when it eventually deposited them on another vehicle track. In fact, without the yellow route markers – often merely bearing the black silhouette of a walking figure with a backpack – it would have been easy to get lost or at least waste time and effort on unnecessary detours.

"The problem is that we're climbing at an angle across the lower slopes of the Eiger and so it's not just a question of taking the steepest route," Jack called back at one point.

Lucy followed close behind him. "Running on these gradients is really going to test our stamina!" she thought with keen anticipation.

After covering about one and a half miles, Jack called for a water stop and they turned to look back the way they had come. Grindelwald now lay basking in sunshine, presided over by the beautiful Wetterhorn and a lower mountain on the right, both now completely clear of cloud.

Jack looked at his map. "I think that must be the Mettenberg," he said, before turning to look in the direction they were travelling. There was not a lot to see apart from the wooded area they would soon enter because there were very few gaps in the clouds that still covered the higher slopes.

They ran on, happily breathing the invigorating air, sometimes single file on a narrow path and sometimes side-by-side on a rough track.

It was not long before they reached a pedestrian gate at the point where the path entered the wood and became much more uneven. Lucy stopped to take out one of her water bottles. "This is thirsty work; I hope I don't run out!" she said.

"There should be an opportunity to refill at Brandegg station where I think there may be a restaurant. Hopefully, we can get some coffee there as well," Jack assured her as they ploughed on.

They eventually emerged on a narrow well-maintained road that took them under the railway line just before it reached the station and a surprisingly large restaurant. Being early in the season, only part of the establishment was in use, but they joined a few other walkers and train travellers.

"This is nice," Lucy said happily as they sipped the rather small cups of black coffee accompanied by tiny capsules of cream. The view down towards Grindelwald was magnificent.

"I guess some people just take the train up here for the view and refreshments," Jack said. "It would also make a splendid walk back because you'd be facing the valley most of the time."

It was not long before they got going again and, after another mile, passed close to Alpiglen station and a small restaurant that was still closed. Every so often a train laboriously climbed up or descended the track that was never far from them.

About a mile later, they stopped for a drink and looked down at Grindelwald once again, nestled in the valley far below them. Then Jack turned back to see if Kleine Scheidegg was in sight.

It was indeed – a few tiny buildings were perched on a ridge less than two miles away – but so much more greeted his astonished gaze. He now realized that they had been so intent on endeavouring to keep up a steady pace and take care of their footing on the rough surface that they had not noticed the change.

"Lucy, turn round!" he commanded.

She did and literally gasped in astonishment; the Eiger, Mönch and Jungfrau were almost completely clear of cloud and a long line of snow-covered mountains stretched out into the distance. She was speechless for a moment.

"Oh, Jack; thank you for bringing us here!" she eventually cried.

"You should be thanking John; he's the one who sent us," Jack replied.

"I know, but you planned our outings," she said and kissed his cheek in her enthusiasm. "That view has filled me with fresh energy; I can run for miles now! Let's get going."

Jack's heart was singing as he followed her up the winding path, not just because of their wonderful surroundings but because his cheek still tingled from the touch of her lips.

......

About 45 minutes later, Lucy and Jack were sitting at a table outside the station restaurant in Kleine Scheidegg having some well-deserved refreshments and watching one of the red Jungfraujoch trains filling up with excited tourists and beginning its steep journey to the escarpment of the magnificent Mönch and Jungfrau. Both mountains towered over 2000m above them and were covered in snow, brilliant in the bright sunlight, except where there were almost vertical faces of grey rock.

"Thankfully we have good sunglasses," Lucy remarked. "I'm surprised the snow is still so close to us in early June."

"It can't be long since the top of the path from Grindelwald was completely clear of snow; indeed we may find some on the way down to Wengen and Lauterbrunnen," Jack responded.

"I love snow!" The normally rather serious Lucy looked as excited as a happy schoolgirl.

......

The route to Wengen followed the railway quite closely and began by going southwest, descending gently at first parallel to the range of mountains Lucy and Jack had followed all morning, even when veiled in cloud. The snow-covered slopes were completely breathtaking when viewed against the backdrop of a pale blue sky and they had to keep stopping just to absorb the sight of the mighty Jungfrau.

Lucy was also delighted when they came across a shallow band of snow blocking the path. Although many hiking boots had worn down a muddy gap, she insisted on carefully climbing across the white surface: melting in the warm sun but still crisp under the soles of her trainers.

After not much more than a mile, the young couple reached Wengernalp station and the surprisingly large chalet-style Hotel Jungfrau. Its shuttered windows were firmly closed.

"I believe the train only stops here on request in the summer; you probably have to wave it down like catching a bus!" Jack commented. "It's too early in the season for the hotel to be open but I expect it was bulging at the seams with skiers last winter."

"Very convenient for the slopes and the winter views must be awesome!" Lucy exclaimed as they stopped for water.

She wandered over the grass and spotted a large patch of deep blue trumpet-shaped flowers. She called Jack over to admire them.

"Those are gentians," he said, "but keep your eyes peeled for alpine roses; they're a sort of miniature rhododendron with clusters of tiny bell-shaped red flowers on a small shrub. We're still above the tree line and should be high enough for them."

They moved on again and found that the wide path curved gradually north away from the Jungfrau and began to drop down sharply.

"It's only three miles to Wengen now. Let's run together; there's plenty of room." Jack said.

......

The track wound its way steeply down and along what appeared to be a wide shelf half way up the eastern side of the Lauterbrunnen valley. To the young couple's right, a high ridge ran all the way from Kleine Scheidegg to the Männlichen, an attractive mountain almost clear of snow towering above Wengen. To their left, a splendid range of mountains on the far side of the valley rose above immense cliffs that surged up out of the valley floor.

At their next water stop, Lucy and Jack could see the small village of Mürren perched on the cliff, backed by the snow-capped Schilthorn.

"Tomorrow, we could come by train to Lauterbrunnen, run to the end of the valley and then up the steep path to Mürren; it's almost eight miles and a climb of 800m," Jack suggested.

"There and back should be no problem at all; I look forward to it!" Lucy responded with a smile of anticipation before they set off again.

Every so often they came within sight or sound of the little green and yellow trains passing slowly to and from Kleine Scheidegg and it was not long before they had a splendid view of the village of Wengen nestling contentedly below the Männlichen.

"We'll have a nice refreshment stop there," Jack said.

......

It seemed no time at all before the young couple were descending through the outskirts of Wengen and following the railway track into the centre. Almost next door to a Coop supermarket, they spotted a small café and thankfully entered.

"Let's just have a large cup of milky coffee here and get some sandwiches from the Coop to eat on one of those benches near the station," Lucy suggested.

Jack nodded. "We'll have a proper meal in Wilderswil tonight but don't forget to refill your water flasks when you visit the loo."

"I'm not likely to forget, given the amount of water I consume when I'm running!" Lucy replied with a short laugh.

......

The descent to the outskirts of Lauterbrunnen was steeper than anything they had experienced so far that day.

"We're going down 500m in the space of two miles and so it's bound to be very steep in places," Jack said at one point when they were forced to go particularly carefully.

"It would be a real challenge to jog up here nonstop," Lucy replied. "I'd love to try it."

"Perhaps the day after tomorrow," Jack said rather hesitantly, not sure if he would be able to keep up with his amazing companion.

The views of the deep Lauterbrunnen valley were certainly impressive, particularly the Staubbach Falls cascading 300m down a cliff face that rose almost vertically from the valley floor. As the young couple neared the village, however, they felt almost hemmed in by the surrounding heights after the gloriously wide open spaces they had left behind.

"Let's keep going on foot and not bother about the train," Jack suggested.

Lucy grinned. "I was hoping you'd suggest that; I've still got plenty of energy left," she said.

They bypassed the centre of Lauterbrunnen and followed the signs to Interlaken. Unfortunately, this entailed running single file on a fairly busy road for over two miles before they were able to join a path.

It was with a real sense of achievement that they entered the homely guesthouse in Wilderswil after their first trail run over a really high mountain pass.

......

71

After refreshing showers and a short rest, Jack and Lucy walked to a nearby restaurant for a meal. They were hungry and so started with a thick vegetable broth called Bündner Gerstensuppe: a delicious mixture of barley, leek, carrot, celery and tiny flakes of dried meat, accompanied by a thick slice of homemade bread.

"We must remember to have this again," Lucy said enthusiastically.

Jack made a quick note of the name, delighted that she looked so pleased. The main course was less successful, but, nevertheless, they walked back to the guesthouse comfortably full and more than ready for a very early night.

......

On Friday morning they boarded the 8:40 to Lauterbrunnen. Jack made sure they were in the front half of the train, in contrast to the previous day when they had been aiming for Grindelwald. Their plan was to run south for four miles up the valley from Lauterbrunnen to the hamlet of Stechelburg and then take a right turn to join the steep path up to Mürren.

The journey was shorter than on the previous day. Within a few minutes of leaving the junction where the train divided, the front portion pulled slowly into Lauterbrunnen.

"The single tickets were cheaper than yesterday and so I should have guessed that the journey would be shorter," Jack commented as they walked south along the village street.

"Train fares are very expensive anyway," Lucy said.

"At least the trains run on time," Jack replied. "It's also possible for visitors to buy a half-price travel card lasting a month but it would not be worth it for the small amount of travelling we're doing."

On the edge of the village, the road curved sharply left to drop down over the river and follow it up the valley. Jack, however, guided them on to a much narrower road that went straight ahead and kept quite close to the amazing cliffs lining the western side of the valley.

"I reckon I could throw a stone and reach the cliff face," Lucy remarked, but this thought was quickly forgotten when she looked further along and saw the Staubbach Falls at close quarters. "Wow!" was all she could mutter.

Jack could even feel the spray as a sudden gust of wind swept a few fine droplets towards them.

"We'll pass several waterfalls but this is the more spectacular, apart perhaps for the Trümmelbach Falls on the other side of the valley where the water has burrowed its way down inside the mountain," he said. "But now we should start running on this almost level surface."

......

At the pace the young couple ran, invigorated by the superb air and scenery, it took them under half an hour to cover the remaining three and a half miles to Stechelburg and a restaurant where they were able to have a cup of coffee at a table under a tree in the small garden before starting the twisting climb to Mürren.

"This is just what we need!" Lucy cried as the gradient became extremely steep.

They passed through the hamlet of Grimmelwald after climbing about 450m over a distance of one and a half miles. Then the gradient eased slightly and the path became wider and very well maintained: clearly now intended for tourists taking a walk from Mürren. The second half of the climb was therefore easier, only going up another 250m.

With a feeling of achievement, the young couple emerged on one of the main streets of the pretty village. After a short sightseeing tour, they found a restaurant with a large terrace and were able to look out across the Lauterbrunnen valley whilst eating an excellent open sandwich. It was a dull day but the clouds were just above the mountain tops and so the view was still good by any measure.

"I found the route up here using Google Maps before we came away but I've just noticed on my walking map that we can go back a different way," Jack said as he munched. "There's a path that follows the narrow gauge railway north along the top of the cliff for just over three miles to the top of a cable lift that goes straight down into Lauterbrunnen. Quite close to the lift we can join a path that winds down over 500m into the village."

"Returning that way will give us a different view of this splendid scenery," Lucy said.

......

The cliff top path followed the railway line fairly closely and they covered the distance extremely quickly, especially given the fact that the wide path was on a slightly downward slope.

They had a short break for water near the top of the cable lift, standing looking over at Wengen on the opposite side of the valley.

"Wengen looks an ideal location for trail running; it would be nice to stay there one day," Jack observed.

This gave Lucy an idea. "Today has been quite an easy one, even given the fact that we've still got a long winding descent ahead of us," she said. "What about coming back to Lauterbrunnen by train again tomorrow and running over to Grindelwald and back? After all, we're going to have to do something similar when we're in Adelboden."

"That'll be a good test of our ability. We could have lunch at that nice restaurant at Brandegg overlooking Grindelwald," Jack replied, hoping that Lucy would not want to go right down into the village.

"I'm looking forward to it," she replied as she put on her rucksack ready for the long descent.

Chapter 9: A Real Challenge

Thus it was that, on their last full day in Wilderswil, Lucy and Jack tackled their greatest challenge so far, helped by the fact that the weather was sunny with a cool breeze. In a way, it was a dress rehearsal for what they would have to do in earnest in three days time.

Lara Geber had been extremely surprised when Jack mentioned their plans at breakfast but she was too polite to comment. A generation ago it would have been unheard of for a girl to undertake such a physically demanding activity.

Lucy, on the other hand, was full of excited anticipation that grew as the train journey progressed. It seemed to be contagious and Jack found himself swept up by her enthusiasm and absolutely determined not to let her down. He would let her set the pace even though he would have to dig deep to keep up.

It was fortunate that the steeper part of the ascent was the first section from Lauterbrunnen up to Wengen when the runners were at their freshest. A slow jog was all that was possible on such a gradient but Lucy showed what she was capable of by doing the 500m climb to the outskirts of the village without stopping. Here they paused briefly for water and a look at the valley they had left behind.

"I knew we could do that climb in one go," she declared.

She looked at Jack. He had kept within two or three yards of her all the way and was now struggling to get his breath back. "Well done!" she added with a congratulatory smile.

He grinned happily at her but did not trust himself to say more than two words, "Coffee break?"

Lucy was about say that they ought to continue immediately but then she relented; they had achieved their objective and the thought of coffee was appealing.

......

The rest of the ten-mile run over Kliene Scheidegg to Brandegg was uneventful but strangely enjoyable despite the exertion: the gradients were less, the weather just right, the air delicious and the views glorious.

A magnificent view also awaited them at the restaurant where they treated themselves to an omelette and cold drink at a table overlooking Grindelwald and the beautiful Wetterhorn. They deliberately took time over coffee to let the meal settle before the return run.

......

A very happy couple settled down thankfully in the Interlaken train as it waited at Lauterbrunnen station for its departure time.

"We've really achieved something today. I think we're ready for the tough run from Adelboden to Kandersteg and back," Lucy said with delight.

Jack smiled fondly at her, so wanting to hug her and wondering if there would be an opportunity later.

As it turned out there would be, but only after the young couple had showered and changed at the guesthouse and then returned to Wilderswil station to catch the train for the short journey to Interlaken Ost.

"Don't we need tickets?" Lucy had asked as they boarded the train.

"No; for short journeys in the Interlaken area, we can use the guest cards Lara gave me when we arrived; you get them because a visitor tax is included in the cost of accommodation."

Arriving at Ost station, they started walking towards the centre of the town but soon found a restaurant with a reasonable menu outside and decided they were too hungry to look any further.

......

Comfortably full and delighted with the day's tough run, Lucy linked arms with her companion as they walked to the

76

bank of the River Aare for one last look at the water in the gathering dusk. Jack glanced down; her normally serious face had never looked so happy and relaxed.

"You're amazing; not only incredibly strong and fit but also a beautiful and delightful companion. I could not have a better girlfriend," he said quietly.

Lucy looked up at him. It was just possible to see her expression in the fading light; it conveyed a mixture of surprise and delight.

"Do you really mean that? ...Yes, I'm sure you do," she murmured, answering her own question.

Jack drew her to him. She made no attempt to resist and their lips met in their first kiss.

They stood completely still, the only sound the water gurgling and splashing its way from one lake to the other.

He was about to release her when she suddenly wrapped her arms around him and kissed him again, her embrace so tight that he could feel the hard muscles of her lithe body pressing against him.

"You've won me over," she said eventually. "No ifs and buts; we really are proper friends now!"

"I only want to make you happy," Jack said, as they turned to go back to the station for the train to Wilderswil. "I never cease to be thankful that I happened to see John's advert in a castoff newspaper and answered it. Otherwise I wouldn't have met a girl far beyond my wildest dreams!"

......

Lara Geber hugged them both when Lucy and Jack left the following morning. "Do come again and stay with us longer next time," she urged. "I'm sure the mountain paths around here are just as good as anything you'll find in Adelboden."

Chapter 10: Adelboden

Almost two hours after leaving Wilderswil, the post bus swung into the dark and cavernous bus terminus in the centre of Adelboden. The young couple thankfully alighted after the rather bouncy ten-mile ride from Frutigen, where they had had to leave the comfortable train from Spiez.

"It's not surprising that the road up here is so steep: Adelboden is about the same height as Wengen," Jack remarked as they walked down the main street. "I suggest we find a place to stay before coming back here for coffee."

Lucy nodded. She was looking around her with interest; this would be the starting point of their great adventure.

Jack had already listed two pensions (guesthouses) from his research on Google Maps. They made their way to the nearer one to view it from the outside.

Lucy looked at it uncertainly. "I'm not sure," she said.

"John has given us enough money to use a hotel if necessary, but we'd be less conspicuous somewhere small on the outskirts of the village," Jack responded. "If you don't mind a walk of just over a mile, my second selection is down the hill and across the river in the direction we'll take when we go over the ridge to Kandersteg.

"At least that would have the advantage of being able to slip out quietly early Tuesday morning without going anywhere near the centre of the village," Lucy said.

"That's one of the reasons I chose it, apart from the fact that it's on a small quiet road," Jack replied with a grin. "Let's see if there's a vacancy."

It was not long before they were standing in the tiny foyer of the pension ringing the bell. A man of about 60 years of age appeared after a moment or two and gave them a beaming smile.

"Guten Tag. Would you like a room? You're in luck. We only opened for the summer season yesterday." He spoke in such rapid colloquial German that Jack only managed to pick up the gist of his words before replying in the same language, saying that they would like a room, en-suite if possible.

......

Lucy was soon looking happily out of the window of a small but comfortable room. A grassy slope dotted with clumps of trees greeted her eyes and a carefully tended window box of red geraniums gave off an attractive scent.

Only one thing worried her; although there were separate mattresses in the large bed frame, there was only one enormous duvet.

Jack was sensitive enough to have noticed. He went over and stood beside her with his arm around her waist. "I love and value you far too much to do anything untoward. I also promise not to hog the duvet!"

She kissed his cheek to show she understood before suggesting they return to the village for coffee and some sandwiches to take with them on an afternoon hike.

"I must get a walking map of the area," Jack said as they descended the stairs.

......

They found a pleasant café in the village centre before going to the ubiquitous Coop for sandwiches and bananas.

The newly acquired map showed an attractive-looking circular walk on the western slopes above the village together with the recommendation that it be done in the anti-clockwise direction.

For some reason, Lucy showed no desire to run and they climbed steadily side-by-side before finding a bench for their sandwich lunch.

Feeling refreshed but not too full, they continued the climb up the wooded slope. After a short distance, a sign on the right-hand side pointed to the entrance of a steep path that went even higher than the route they were following.

"That might make a lovely run for one of our days here," Lucy said.

"There's an even tougher hike-cum-run that we can try; I'll be able to show you when we reach the viewpoint mentioned on the map," Jack said.

Lucy was, of course, intrigued by the mention of something that sounded like a serious challenge.

......

The viewpoint provided splendid views, not only of Adelboden spread out far below them but also something of even greater interest. From their vantage point, the young couple could now see the layout at the head of the valley.

Over two miles further south, the floor of the wide valley surged up to form the edge of a hanging valley embraced by a semi-circular chain of small mountains, all of modest height compared with the snow-covered peaks in the more distant background.

Jack pointed. "That's what I wanted to show you; it's called Engstligenalp," he said. "It can be reached either by cable car or steep path – no need to guess which you would prefer! Apparently there are a couple of restaurants up there, but before you get to them there's a path that branches off and takes you even higher on to the surrounding ridge. Weather permitting, I suggest we tackle that run tomorrow, although the ridge itself may turn out to be a bit of a scramble because the map doesn't indicate how good the path is!"

"That'll be an excellent outing for tomorrow; a good prelude to D-day!" Lucy agreed with eager anticipation.

......

That evening, they discovered a small restaurant quite close to the pension for their evening meal and were pleased to find that Bündner Gerstensuppe was on the menu: the thick vegetable broth they had so enjoyed in Wilderswil. This was followed by fried trout fillets and rice with white-wine cream sauce.

80

"That was a delicious meal," Lucy commented as they walked back to the guesthouse, "but, at those prices, we'll run out of money before next Thursday!"

"We'll find somewhere cheaper in the village tomorrow," Jack promised.

"I also suggest we get a few simple things like rolls, cheese, tomatoes etc. to have in our bedroom on Tuesday night after getting back from Kandersteg," Lucy added.

They had an early night to prepare for the arduous days to come.

......

Jack set a fast pace for the two-mile run along the road to the cable station at the base of the Engstligenalp escarpment. Lucy followed his lead quite happily, knowing full well that he would want her to take over once they began to climb in earnest.

Arriving at a large car park serving both the cable station and a nearby restaurant, Jack paused to view the impressive escarpment they were about to climb. The top cable station was just visible as a small dark square and, further to the right, they could see the Engstligen Falls cascading down to supply a narrow river hurrying along the valley to join the larger River Allenbach near Adelboden.

"Impressive," was Lucy's only comment.

Turning to run on again, Jack spotted a narrow path disappearing through the trees. "I think this is the way," he called as he sped onwards.

The path through the woods climbed very gently at first but soon the gradient increased sharply. Jack slowed to a jog and glanced back at Lucy.

"Time for my super-fit girlfriend to take over and show me what she's really made of!" he said with a broad grin.

"Huh, any more comments like that and I'll run you into the ground – literately!" came the reply as Lucy accelerated past him.

Fortunately, she soon settled down to a steady jog. Even so, Jack's only respite came when she called for a water stop about half way up.

The left turn off the main path was clearly signposted. Another short stiff climb and the young couple arrived on the 2,100m ridge, having climbed nearly 800m since leaving Adelboden.

Jack was desperately trying to get his breath back and even Lucy was bending over breathing heavily as she reached for her water bottle.

"We're now well over twice the height of Sgurr Fhuaran, the highest of the Five Sisters of Kintail," Jack said eventually, "and, as we scramble along this superb ridge, we'll be going up another 500m!"

"I had no idea it would be so good up here. It was a brilliant idea to come," Lucy said as she looked around.

"The waitress at breakfast said we'd love it," Jack replied, pleased with her reaction.

Lucy led the way forward, no longer interested in covering the ground as quickly as possible but almost savouring every step. It was the same for Jack but he had the added pleasure of watching the girl he loved delighting in her surroundings.

They climbed steadily for about a mile. In places it almost seemed as if they were balancing precariously on a knife edge so steeply did the ground fall away on both sides of the ridge. At first, they appeared to be aiming for a strange-looking mountain crowned with several jagged fingers pointing skywards but the path passed some distance below the summit and continued for another glorious mile as it gradually swung southwest towards the mighty snow-capped Steghorn and Wildstrubel: the two mountains that give the Adelboden valley its dramatic backdrop.

"I feel I could almost reach out and touch that mountain," Lucy said at one point when they emerged from behind a rocky outcrop and the Steghorn came into view again.

Jack laughed. "It's probably about two miles away as the crow flies!"

Lucy grinned at him and his heart did a flip. "At times like this, I wish I could fly!" she said almost wistfully.

......

Even given their deliberately slow progress, made even slower now by the occasional patches of snow, it was not very long before they came to a place where the path ran alongside a massive outcrop of rock that towered almost menacingly above their heads. Then they spotted a welcome signpost.

"I think this is the point where the path we're following crosses a gap in the ridge called Chindbettipass and drops down into the next valley. The path branching off to our right goes back down into Engstligenalp. We could return that way and get some refreshments at one of the restaurants," Jack said after consulting his map.

"Let's go a short distance down into the next valley first," Lucy said, eager to see as much as possible. "Anyway, a place with such an odd name is too intriguing to miss!"

Two minutes later, they went through the gap in the ridge and began the steep descent. Now that they were gazing directly down, the valley looked rather barren and uninteresting apart for a small lake.

"Engstligenalp is much nicer," Lucy commented. "Without the splendid mountain backdrop, this valley would look completely uninviting. Let's go back."

......

They were soon descending the winding path into the basin of the hanging valley. There had been surprisingly few hikers on the ridge itself but now there were plenty taking the direct route from the restaurants to photograph the views from Chindbettipass, as Jack had done before leaving the ridge. In fact, he was secretly delighted to have managed to capture a side view of camera-shy Lucy gazing pensively at the Steghorn and Wildstrubel.

The young couple had run two and a half miles and descended over 500m by the time they passed an attractive looking restaurant called Berghaus Bärtschi.

"I think we deserve coffee and something to eat," Jack said firmly

Lucy needed no persuading. "Just lead me to it," she replied.

It was only when they were sitting at a table in the pleasant building that they realized it was also a small hotel. "I expect the accommodation is mainly used during the skiing season," Lucy surmised.

Their refreshment break did not take very long and they were careful to replenish their empty water flasks before leaving to tackle the steep descent into the main valley. Lucy led the way but took the slope very steadily; they could not afford a twisted ankle so close to their big day.

Near the bottom of the path, Jack spotted a sign to the Engstligen Falls and called out with a suggestion.

"Let's make a detour to see the Falls at close quarters, although I think it will be from fairly near the bottom. My map shows that we can then take a path that emerges on the road to Adelboden a short distance north of the lower cable station."

"A good idea," Lucy said as she came back to join him. To his delight, she took his hand and they walked together full of anticipation at what they were about to witness.

They were not disappointed. An immense volume of water gushed over the top of the escarpment and crashed down towards them sending out plumes of spray. They could almost feel the tremor as the torrent pummelled any rocks that dared to impede its descent.

"Wow!" Lucy and Jack exclaimed almost in unison. They looked at each other and grinned.

"Now for an energetic run back to the guesthouse for a shower and then on into the village for some shopping and a meal," Lucy added after a pause, almost reverting to her trainer mode.

Jack did not mind in the least; he was so pleased she was enjoying the day.

Chapter 11: D-Day

By now Jack had made friends with the elderly owner of the pension. Unlike the talkative waitress who delighted in practicing her language skills, the man spoke very little English and Jack was only too pleased to chat to him in German.

Thus it was that the young couple were allowed to come down at 6:30, half an hour before the breakfast room normally opened. They had to miss out on a boiled egg but there was a good choice of cereals, ham, processed meat and cheese, not to mention the delicious homemade bread.

......

"I'll start by jogging slowly so that we don't get indigestion but then speed up until the gradient increases," Lucy said as they set off at 7:15 prompt. It had been agreed that she would lead the way to the top of the pass and Jack take over on the descent.

It was only occasionally necessary to stop to consult the map because the route was well signposted. Nevertheless, the young couple were quite surprised how far they had to run on a mixture of narrow roads and paths before the gradients became really serious and even Lucy was forced to a slow jog. At their occasional water stops, the views up and down the Adelboden valley were splendid despite the mist that clung to all the high mountains.

Eventually, they passed a small restaurant – still closed – at Bunderalp. "That might be useful on the way back," Lucy called rather breathlessly over her shoulder.

They jogged over peaceful meadows on a winding path getting gradually closer to contorted rock formations that gave the impression of having sprouted almost arbitrarily from the formidable ridge separating the two valleys.

When they next stopped for water, they were able to clearly see the V-shaped notch that was their objective.

"That's the Bunderchrinde Pass," Jack announced. "At 2360m, it's about 200m lower than the surrounding peaks in the ridge."

"I can see some patches of snow; I hope they don't delay us too much. And what's that grey stuff?" Lucy asked.

"Shale scree eroded from the rock face; the map mentions that it may be unstable and slippery."

As the result of this warning, Lucy led the way gingerly across the large area. The path was often barely visible but at least they knew their destination. Several detours were necessary, mainly due to the thin patches of icy snow that made the surface even more hazardous.

......

It was with considerable relief that the young couple breasted the gap and caught their first glimpse of the Kandersteg valley. By any measure it was an impressive view. Kandersteg nestled far below them and, further east, a lake glinted in the sunlight, presided over by a high mountain.

"That's the Blüelisalphorn. It looks enormous but is actually about 400m lower than the Jungfrau," Jack said, pausing for a moment before he began to lead the way down the switchback of a path. "We're in fairly good time, even allowing for the delay over the shale and snow, so I'll take it carefully on the really steep bits of this descent."

"That'll make it easier on our thighs," Lucy agreed.

"Those splendid thighs could cope with anything!" Jack thought fondly.

......

The winding path was steeper on this side of the ridge and the views even more breathtaking, although this may have been partly due to the direction the runners were facing.

Eventually, they found themselves in a meadow dominated by looming cliffs and were surprised to pass a small restaurant where several people were enjoying refreshments.

Jack stopped for a few mouthfuls of water. "It would be nice to have a proper drink here but I'm not sure how much further we've got to go," he remarked sadly.

They ploughed on and went down a long path beside a rushing stream in a narrow gorge followed by a wider path alongside a river. The route was almost level by now and, when they finally entered a road running parallel to the railway track, they knew their journey was nearly over.

They were entering Kandersteg from the south and Jack stopped to look at a sketch map of the village centre that he extracted from beside the precious manuscript in his rucksack.

"We need to go north until we reach the station and then turn left. The café is part of the Hotel zur Post that should be almost facing us when we get to the main street," he reported.

"Don't forget to hide the manuscript inside that newspaper you bought yesterday before we go in," Lucy warned him.

"Thanks for the reminder. I've only brought the outer three pages so that the final package is not too thick."

The young couple reached the station sooner than they had expected. It overlooked a pleasant park fringed by small trees and the road leading to the main street was directly in front of them. The whole place was surprisingly flat compared with the other mountain villages they had visited and seemed to be almost completely enclosed by mountains of varying heights.

Jack spied the station café. "It's only 12:40. We've got time for coffee," he said.

"Not to mention a visit to the loo!" Lucy chuckled, surveying the attractive scene.

......

The welcoming wooden interior of the Hotel zur Post's café-restaurant was fairly small and quite popular. In fact, Lucy and Jack were lucky to find an empty table near the door. As they settled into their seats, Jack casually laid his folded newspaper on the side of the table nearer to the narrow walkway.

While they consulted the menu, Lucy looked around surreptitiously. Two men, clearly regular customers judging by the way they were chatting to a waitress, were at a table a short distance away; one of them wore a rather faded salmon-pink shirt.

"He's here," Lucy whispered very quietly, her heart racing with excitement.

The waitress came to take their order. Jack selected something nourishing but not too heavy for both of them and two cold drinks. He spoke in German in the hope that, although they were bound to be recognized as foreigners, it might not be obvious that they were British. As the waitress was leaving the table, she spoke again briefly.

"She's just said that, having ordered a main course, we can help ourselves to the salad bar near the serving counter," Jack explained quietly when she was out of earshot. "I can hardly hold the package under my arm, so you'd better go first and I'll get something quickly when you get back."

Lucy was quick and it was not long before they both had bowls of salad and the very welcome cold drinks that had just appeared.

"I'm hungry. May I start nibbling?" Lucy asked.

"Of course you may," Jack replied. "In this part of the world it's looked upon as the starter course."

......

They had just started on the main meal when the man in the salmon-pink shirt made his move. He was obviously working together with his friend because the latter was leading the way out when he suddenly stopped at the table opposite Lucy and Jack to engage the occupants in brief conversation. This gave "pink shirt" the excuse to squeeze past, almost brushing Jack's elbow as he deftly scooped up the package and left a small brown envelop in its place.

No words were spoken but Lucy thought she detected a very faint "Danke".

The two young people looked at each other, taking care not to register relief or any other emotion that might be noted by an observant customer. Solemnly, they continued with their meal.

As they finished eating, Jack spoke for the first time in several minutes.

"If we were normal visitors, I would suggest a three-mile trip to see the famous "Blue Lake" and then returning to Adelboden by public transport. However, John wanted us to leave Kandersteg as quickly and quietly as possible: so we'd better slip away as soon as you're ready."

"I suppose he was worried that the village, or possibly the businessman's chalet, might be under observation. Anyway, all our training has been to tackle the double run and I'm looking forward to it," Lucy responded.

Jack nodded. "Now that I come to think of it, we should've steered well clear of the station on our way in."

"Not to mention the station café!" Lucy said. "I wasn't thinking straight either."

"Well, I'll make sure we avoid it on our way out," Jack promised as he switched on his smartphone and tapped in a simple two word message to the number John had given him.

"Mission accomplished!" it read.

......

The climb out of Kandersteg was appreciably steeper than on the Adelboden side but Lucy and Jack did not care; they felt so buoyed up by their success.

By the time they arrived back at the Adelboden pension, however, it was a different matter. Even Lucy was ready to acknowledge that she should have done less running and more walking on the climb up to Bunderchrinde, because they had then had to cope with the slippery shale and snow followed by a long thigh-taxing descent.

Even climbing the stairs to their bedroom was quite an effort and they both collapsed on the bed for a rest before they could even contemplate a shower or eating the rather meagre provisions bought the previous day.

"I'm really glad we don't have to go out again," Jack said at one point.

They slept so soundly that they were almost late for breakfast.

Chapter 12: Danger Lurks

Lucy and Jack's jubilation at mission accomplished returned in full measure at the breakfast table.

"Let's do something less strenuous today; I need to unwind!" Lucy said as she spread a generous portion of butter on a slice of wholemeal bread containing tiny pieces of nut.

Jack looked at her in surprise; was this really Lucy speaking? Nevertheless, he was grateful because he felt the same.

"I know you like wild flowers. There's something called the Adelboden Flower Trail several miles southwest of Adelboden; it's said to be very popular and even has picture boards to illustrate the different plants," he replied. "There's a cable lift that goes up there about two miles from here, although it's probably quite expensive. Alternatively, we could do a circular tour of 15 miles or so, but some of it would have to be by road."

"Normally I'd jump at the opportunity to do something like that," Lucy said slowly. "However, I'd prefer to have our last day to ourselves somewhere less touristy."

Jack looked at her in pleased surprise for the second time that morning, trying to conceal the fact that his heart was beating faster. All he really wanted to do was to spend quality time with the girl he loved. An idea came to mind.

"You remember our first outing here on the western slopes above Adelboden?" he said. "Some distance before the viewpoint where I pointed out Engstligenalp, we passed a steep path that went much higher. We should be able to find some alpine flowers up there if we go high enough."

He opened the walking map again. "Yes, here we are. The path eventually reaches Schwandfeldspitz and Tschenten Alp, both about 600m above Adelboden."

Lucy followed his finger as it traced the route. "What a splendid idea!" she exclaimed. "It'll be great fun to go well above the tree line again and do some hunting. There should be some splendid views as well. We could even take sandwiches up there."

Jack nodded happily.

......

Little more than an hour later, the young couple were jogging slowly up the familiar narrow road out of the centre of Adelboden. Jack was happy; not only was there no need to use the map but he had the pleasure of watching his companion's strong legs carrying her almost effortlessly upwards. There was no sign that, only the previous day, her stamina had been tested almost to its limit, not to mention his!

It was not long before they left the main path to climb through a dense wood of spruce, larch and pine trees. Lucy was forced to slow down. She soon stopped altogether and turned to Jack, holding out her hand invitingly.

"Let's climb together," she said, giving him a warm smile of invitation.

Jack needed no further encouragement to clasp her hand firmly. Such was his euphoric state of mind that even the path seemed to exude a sense of adventure as it zigzagged up the slope. Every so often, a shaft of sunlight broke through the foliage to bathe the thick carpet of conifer needles in a warm glow.

Eventually, the trees thinned and they emerged into bright sunlight. After another steep climb they found themselves in a high alpine meadow. The hardy grass, recently released from its icy captivity, was dotted with a profusion of flowers.

"Look at all those little mauve thistles and the delicate flowers that look like small primroses," Lucy said with delight.

"And those clusters of tiny pale blue flowers thriving in the crevices of that rock," added Jack, indicating a jagged slab of granite that was clearly part of the bedrock that lay below the meagre layer of soil.

They moved on, climbing gradually higher whilst looking carefully on both sides of the path.

Suddenly, Lucy gave a cry. "I can see some clumps of blue about ten yards to the right."

They made their way carefully over and discovered twenty or so vibrant gentians scattered over the ground, their delicate trumpets shimmering in the light breeze.

"If I ever get a dress, it'll certainly be that amazing colour if possible," Lucy declared.

"It would most certainly suit you," Jack said, looking at her with undisguised admiration.

The girl blushed, uncertain how to react. "Let's find a rock to sit on and have our sandwiches. I'm famished!" she suggested, endeavouring to cover her confusion.

Before long, they were perched on an uncomfortable slab of rock munching happily and taking in the superb mountain scenery.

......

It was only as they were standing up again that Jack glanced a short distance behind them. His eyes were greeted by several tiny pale red flowers on a small bush reminiscent of a miniature rhododendron – it was an alpine rose.

"Found one at last!" he exclaimed. "I looked out for them at Wengernalp without success."

Lucy crouched down beside him to admire the small plant. "It's lovely but I think I prefer gentians," she said. "Let's carry on and keep a lookout for both."

They walked on and were finally rewarded with another possible sighting a few yards to the left. Stepping carefully over, they discovered that it was indeed an alpine rose, but a rather poor specimen.

"They sometimes grow in clusters, so keep searching in this vicinity," Jack instructed.

It was whilst doing so that Lucy observed a solitary woman walking slowly past in the direction of Tschenten Alp.

She would have thought no more of it if the woman had not been wearing a heavy grey tweed suit and looking extremely uncomfortable on such a warm sunny day.

Lucy nudged Jack to get his attention and they looked at the woman's retreating back for a moment or two. They were, however, completely taken aback when she suddenly swung round and peered back at them through a small pair of binoculars.

"How odd," Lucy murmured. "Is she a birdwatcher, do you think?"

"I very much doubt it," Jack replied uneasily as he quickly pretended to be looking for flowers again. "It's just possible she's a mafia spy. We could have been spotted in Kandersteg yesterday afternoon when we set out to run back here; it would have been virtually impossible for anyone to catch up with us but pretty obvious our destination was Adelboden."

Lucy looked surprised but unconcerned; no mere woman would get the better of her.

"It's a good job the manuscript has been safely delivered," she said, "but how on earth do they know what we look like?"

"The only thing I can think of is that the Bodleian informer may have sent them a picture of us, perhaps taken from the CCTV camera at the reception desk when we went to collect the package. As a result, somebody's been watching out for us in Kandersteg for the last few days and may even have called up reinforcements. I wish we hadn't gone anywhere near the station," Jack said as he took his companion's elbow and encouraged her back towards the path.

"But why not just keep watch on the chalet itself? It would have been so much easier," Lucy asked.

"Perhaps the wretched mole didn't know the intended recipient but managed to glean the information that he lives somewhere in or near Kandersteg. Anyway, I suggest we walk up to the woman and politely ask her what she wants," Jack replied.

By now, the binoculars were back in the woman's large shoulder bag and she was speaking urgently into a mobile 'phone.

However, when the young couple reached the path and turned towards her, she delved into the bag again with her spare hand. When it emerged, it was holding a small handgun.

Chapter 13: Miraculous Escape

"That puts a new complexion on things," Lucy said quietly.

Jack immediately stepped in front of her to act as a shield. "She can hardly shoot us on a public footpath, especially as there are three teenage girls about 150 yards behind her and coming this way," he said reassuringly.

"The book...where...is it?" the woman called, struggling with an unfamiliar language.

She waved the gun menacingly before remembering to glance over her shoulder to see if anyone was coming.

"I've no idea what you're talking about," Jack said, spreading his hands in a gesture of ignorance.

The woman was obviously flustered by the sight of the approaching trio. She gestured with the gun, making it obvious that she wanted them to go back towards Adelboden.

"Walk!" she said.

"We'd better do what she wants," Jack said reluctantly.

They turned and walked away with the woman following a few yards behind.

......

Before long, Lucy and Jack began to increase speed. The woman could be heard breathing heavily in her attempt to keep up.

"Slower!" she called eventually, torn between her exhaustion and the fact that the teenagers were slowly catching them all up. Jack's surreptitious glance revealed that the handgun was no longer in view.

"I suggest we very gradually speed up again," he whispered. "With luck, by the time we reach the long zigzag in the woods, we'll be far enough ahead to be out of sight for a few seconds and have an opportunity to slip off the path and hide."

Lucy nodded her understanding. Jack thought he heard a faint "Good thinking!" and felt a surge of affection for this girl who was showing no sign of fear or panic.

There and then, he came to a decision. Tonight, after they were safely back in Adelboden, he would ask Lucy to marry him. This new determination, coming after days of taking their relationship so very cautiously, filled him with strength and courage. He felt ready to fight giants to protect Lucy, let alone an out-of-condition woman with a gun!

They had speeded up appreciably during his time of reflection and he was surprised to find that they had reached the relative cover of the trees and begun the twisting descent through the increasingly dense conifer wood.

The gap between them and the woman had widened, apparently unnoticed by her because no further gruff command had been issued. This may have been partly due to the fact that an elderly man had just appeared a short distance away climbing up in the opposite direction.

He passed them with a friendly greeting and continued on towards the woman. "We couldn't endanger him by getting him involved," Lucy muttered, almost to herself.

Meanwhile, Jack had been trying to puzzle out the woman's eventual intention for them when the word "sheepdog" suddenly popped into his head. Yes, that was it; she was shepherding them into some form of trap!

The gradient increased significantly and the path began to zigzag down the slope in much longer loops.

"Anytime now we'll be out of sight. Get ready," Lucy said quietly. "Hopefully, she'll pass us and then we can run back towards Tschenten Alp. There must be another way back to Adelboden and she hasn't got a hope of keeping up with us!"

Although the conifers were densely packed, their lower branches were sparse and provided limited ground cover over the short distance between adjacent legs of the path. Approaching the next bend, however, they saw that a semi-circular embankment had been built up around its outer corner to create a small flat area intended for the temporary storage of logs, judging by the few that still lay there.

This was their opportunity.

Jack took Lucy's hand and they sped almost silently over to the far end and stepped over the edge. Not only was the bank steep but the carpet of pine needles very slippery and they found themselves slithering down almost out of control until their heels landed on a rocky ledge. It was only then that they discovered this narrow ledge had saved them from slipping over the edge of an almost vertical rock face.

Breathing sighs of relief, they turned over so that their toes were able get a firmer hold. Surprisingly, they had not slipped all that far. Lucy found she was just able to peer between the tufts of long coarse grass edging the storage area. Jack's head, on the other hand, was completely exposed.

They were only just in time.

Jack had to duck down quickly as the woman appeared around the corner of the path about a dozen yards away and came towards them. She was followed a few seconds later by the three teenage girls.

The woman passed the storage area and turned the corner to go down the next leg of the path. Immediately, two angry male voices broke the silence; the woman must have run into the colleagues summoned earlier and was now being accused of losing their quarry.

The girls rounded the same bend and the noise ceased abruptly while the arguing group waited for them to pass and get out well of earshot.

Lucy looked at Jack; the situation was now serious. They had virtually no chance of extracting themselves from this awkward spot quietly enough to escape up the path before the armed thugs forced them to stop. Yet to stay in their present hiding place risked almost certain detection if the gang start a serious search.

Jack, however, smiled reassuringly at her. He was still buoyed up by his earlier decision and determined to protect the girl he loved, even to the extent of giving himself up so that she might have a chance to escape. He reasoned that the thugs would probably be satisfied to capture him alone. But there was something he must try to do first during the brief breathing space provided by the girls; namely contact the police.

A mere eight days ago, back in Carlisle, John had written his mobile telephone number on a small white card that had been lying discarded on the café table. After arriving in Interlaken, Jack had added the separate Swiss emergency numbers for the police and ambulance services.

At this critical moment high above Adelboden, however, the three-digit numbers were all mixed up in his head. He extracted the card from his hip pocket only for it to escape his awkward grasp and fall a few inches from Lucy's nose.

Instead of telephone numbers, her eyes were greeted by a beautifully printed sentence. She held the card so that they could both see more clearly.

"Everyone who calls on the name of the Lord will be saved (Romans 10:13)," it stated.

It may only have been a trick of the light filtering through the trees but the words appeared to stand out from the white surface as if demanding their attention.

Even in this stressful situation, Lucy found herself recalling the times she had gone to church with her foster-parents and she seemed to know with complete certainty that the Lord being referred to was Jesus Christ.

"We need a miracle," she whispered. "Will you join me in asking Jesus to do what this verse promises?"

Jack looked at her; he had never seen her look so serious or determined. "OK," he murmured.

He gripped the hand holding the little card just as they heard the ominous sound of renewed voices followed by footsteps.

"Lord...Jesus...please...save us!" Their faint words came out in a jumble as they ducked down as far as possible without tumbling off the ledge.

......

Unknown to the hiding couple, the men had divided the task of searching by each taking one side of the upper path while the woman kept watch a little further down in case their quarry escaped again.

Lucy and Jack were only aware of heavy footsteps approaching the storage area and guessed that one of the men was about to check the embankment.

The footsteps came closer. Looking sideways with their cheeks pressed against the bank, they glimpsed the end of a walking pole brushing the clumps of coarse grass to one side.

They closed their eyes, held their breath and waited.

Lucy felt the tip of the long pole brush the top of her head and Jack was hit by a piece of dislodged gravel.

But instead of the expected command to climb out at the point of a gun, the footsteps moved on and finally returned to the main path.

The young couple, their hearts still racing, began breathing normally again. Jack even risked a quick peek over the top of the bank. To his immense relief, he saw the backs of two men moving up the path searching as they went. One of them held a gun.

He ducked down again in case one of the men looked back as they turned the corner.

Lucy looked at him, her eyes wide with astonishment. "That really was a miracle; he must have looked straight at us without seeing us!" she said. "Look! His stick brushed the top of my head and even left a lump of dirt behind."

She extracted the latter from some strands of hair and showed it to her companion.

"You're certainly right about a miracle," Jack replied. "I must start taking Christianity seriously, but now we need to get back to Adelboden as quickly as possible and alert the police, although we can hardly explain why we're the only people these thugs are after!"

They climbed out on to level ground and began to run down the path. It was only when they almost bumped into a middle-aged couple climbing slowly up in the opposite direction that they remembered the woman. Where was she now?

They soon found out. Rounding the next bend, they saw her sitting on a bench a short distance away.

"I've never hit a woman before," Jack said quietly as he stepped in front of his companion.

"I'll be happy to do it!" Lucy exclaimed. "She started all this!"

But it was not necessary. The startled woman rose to her feet and reached into her shoulder bag for the gun. As soon as she gripped it, however, every muscle in her body froze. It was exactly as if the astonished young couple were staring at a waxwork figure, albeit in a most unusual pose.

They took a second to recover before thankfully hurrying on their way. The terrified woman's eyes followed them, seemingly pleading for help. But, when they were some distance away, she could be heard almost shrieking into her 'phone as she desperately summoned her companions.

"At least she's still alive," Lucy said, feeling quite sorry for her. "Perhaps they'll give up trying to find us."

"I guess the men are made of sterner stuff and, of course, they've no idea that this is the second time we've been miraculously rescued," Jack reminded her. "Anyway, we must really get moving."

Lucy nodded and set a fast, almost dangerous, pace back into the centre of the village given that the gradient was still fairly steep.

Chapter 14: A Night to Remember

The Tourist Information Centre in Adelboden could not have been more helpful. They were so shocked at such a thing happening in their law-abiding village that a young man was even delegated to take Jack and Lucy to the police station.

Of course, Jack carefully avoided all reference to anything associated with the manuscript. All he reported was that a woman with a handgun had threatened them near Tschenten Alp, forcing them to go back the way they had come until they managed to escape and hide in the woods just before she was joined by two men, at least one of whom was also armed.

The sole policeman on duty was clearly out of his depth and immediately made an urgent call to his superiors. When it ended, he turned to the helpful young man and spoke rapidly in German. Jack only picked up a few words but the young man translated.

"An armed police unit will be here in less than an hour," he reported. "The officer in charge will want to interview you briefly before the search begins, but, in the meantime, he wants you to describe the people involved to the station officer here and where you last saw them."

By the time Jack and Lucy had supplied the details requested, they were thirsty and hungry. Their stalwart helper, who had to get back to work anyway, guided them to the nearest café after they had promised to return to the police station within half an hour.

It was not a very relaxing break but at least they returned feeling slightly refreshed and ready for another interview. A police car shot round the corner and pulled up sharply just as they were about to enter the building. There were four policemen inside but only one got out, obviously quite senior judging by the more elaborate insignia on his shoulder straps. The car then sped away, presumably to commence the search.

"Guten Tag," the man said as he followed them in and immediately switched to English. "Are you the couple who reported that you had been accosted by a woman with a gun?"

"Yes, we are," Jack replied. "We've described all we can about the woman to the station officer. She was later joined by two men but I only saw their back view from where we were hiding; one has blonde hair and the other almost black. They were both wearing dark green anoraks and grey trousers. The woman has a gun and so does at least one of the men."

By this time, they had arrived in an office where a large map of the area was displayed on the wall. Jack first pointed to the approximate location of their first contact with the woman and then managed to pinpoint where they had managed to hide and eventually escape.

"The woman was pretty exhausted by this time and so stayed close to this location while the two men started to search higher up the path," he said.

The officer immediately began to issue instructions into his radio and listened to the crackling reply before turning to the waiting couple to ask the question they had been hoping to avoid.

"If these people are simply muggers, why did they start searching for you after you escaped? You don't look like wealthy tourists."

Lucy looked at Jack, hoping he would come up with a fairly convincing reply. The latter pretended to look puzzled.

"They seemed to think we had something they wanted," he said slowly. "All that the woman said in broken English while she waved the gun at us was, "The book...where is it?"". Then, because three teenage girls were getting closer, she gestured for us to go back towards Adelboden and followed a short distance behind. Down in the wood, we gradually increased the distance between us so that by the time we reached the main zigzag we were out of sight for a few seconds and managed to hide.

"As soon as she passed our hiding place and turned the corner, we heard her meet the two men and realized she had been trying to drive us into their arms. They argued heatedly and then the men came back up the path searching for us. I can only assume they mistook us for somebody else. We're not carrying a book of any description, but the woman never got to the point of searching our rucksacks and so they probably still think we have whatever they're after."

"We're travelling light and don't have any books in our bedroom either," Lucy said. "Oh, except for a small New Testament my foster parents gave me. I take it with me when I travel anywhere."

This was a surprise to Jack, but then he remembered how fond Lucy was of the couple who had looked after her so well.

The policeman still looked puzzled but merely proceeded to make a note of their local address, Jack's home address and the fact that they were flying back to England the following day and leaving Adelboden at about nine o'clock.

"Thank you for your help," he said. "I expect you're anxious to get on with the remainder of your holiday. If possible, we'll let you know the outcome of our search before you leave."

......

It was six-thirty by the time the young couple finally left the police station and walked back to their modest accommodation. It was a relief to reach the familiar bedroom after such a dramatic interruption to what was supposed to be a happy and restful day to celebrate the success of their mission. Jack was determined to do his best to remedy the situation.

"I'm sorry our happy day on the heights has been spoiled but what about having a celebration dinner at that nice restaurant we visited on our first evening here?" he suggested.

"The food was excellent but wasn't it too expensive?" Lucy asked, although he noticed that she had brightened up at the thought.

"I still have sufficient Swiss francs. I've paid the bill here and we only need to keep some for the fare to Spiez tomorrow and refreshments at the airport," he said. "I already have the return tickets from Interlaken for the rest of the journey to Basle."

"Then a celebration meal would be really nice!" Lucy exclaimed. "Do you mind if I have first shower and then I'll see if I have anything fit to wear."

Jack smiled and nodded. "She'll look marvellous in my eyes whatever she's wearing," he thought fondly.

......

The two-course dinner they enjoyed was just as good, if not better, than it had been the previous time and Lucy was pleased that her favourite Swiss soup was on the menu again. Jack, for his part, basked in the pleasure of watching her enjoy the meal with her usual solemn concentration. In fact, this was another thing that endeared her to him: everything she did, including eating, was done carefully and thoughtfully.

She refused a desert under the pretext of restricting her sugar intake but he suspected that it was because the prices were eye-watering to someone used to careful budgeting.

However, they did treat themselves to cups of the best coffee they had had so far in Switzerland and sipped slowly in contented appreciation of the splendid meal and their successful mission the previous day.

Rather to his surprise, Jack's enjoyment of the meal had not been spoiled by any apprehension about what he was determined to do. In fact, he felt amazingly confident. Could it be Lucy's fleeting glances and little smiles that were boosting his courage? She had hardly said anything but something in way she looked at him was different.

He drew a quiet deep breath. "Lucy," he said slowly.

She smiled at him enquiringly.

"You already know that I think you're amazing; not only super strong and fit with the body of a perfect athlete, but also

106

the best possible companion and partner. You've probably also realized by now that I'm in love with you. In fact, I never thought it possible to love anyone as much as I love you. I'd do anything to make you really happy. Now that we've finished the job assigned to us and are returning home, I want to ask you something."

He stopped abruptly; a lump had suddenly formed in his throat. Only at this last moment did he have the awful thought that she might say no. Then he saw the look on Lucy's face and took heart.

"Lucy; will you marry me?" he asked quietly.

Tears filled the girl's eyes as she gave him the most wonderful smile he had ever seen. She reached out and squeezed the hand close to her.

"Yes," was all she could murmur, but it was quite enough to flood Jack's heart with greater joy than he had ever known.

It was a few moments before she could control her voice sufficiently to add: "Let's get married as soon as possible with the minimum of fuss."

It was now Jack's turn to be speechless and he merely nodded enthusiastically, gulped the remainder of his coffee and paid the bill in a euphoric daze, so eager was he to get Lucy alone.

Once they were a short distance from the restaurant and had found an inconspicuous place, they clung together in one long marvellous kiss before linking arms and walking dreamily back to the pension by the light of the occasional street lamp.

It was only when back in the bedroom that they suddenly felt slightly awkward.

Jack longed to make love to his new fiancée but so deep were his feelings for her that he was determined to be very cautious and make her wishes his top priority. He looked in her direction but she was just disappearing into the bathroom.

......

In the bathroom, Lucy had time to reflect. She had experienced several almost seismic changes over the last few days.

First, and almost to her chagrin, she had found herself beginning to appreciate the company of a man instead of regarding all young males as the opposition, only to be tolerated if they were doing something useful; secondly, Jack's tenderness and understanding when she had unburdened herself on their last night in the Scottish Highlands had gone a long way to melting her previously stony heart; thirdly, she had been swept up in a totally unexpected surge of affection when she had hugged him on that memorable evening on the bank of the River Aare. Since then, her love for Jack had continued to grow steadily.

Now, and by no means least, Jack had been a rock of calmness and stability over the last two days challenging days, even when confronted with a woman armed with a gun. Lucy recalled how he had twice stepped in front of her as a protective shield. As someone used to standing on her own two feet, she had been surprised at her readiness to follow his lead. He had only hesitated once – the time they realized to their horror that they were about to be discovered – and she had then been the one to urge that they should take the words on the little white card at their face value.

All this had turned out to be preparation for her final capitulation. Throughout the celebration dinner, she had known deep down that this was the night of decision.

Then something, or someone, seemed to tell her that he was indeed the one for her. The instant he proposed, joy almost overwhelmed her and their loving kiss beside the road afterwards confirmed her decision many times over.

But would he now expect her to jump into bed with him? She was not sure if she was ready for that. She brushed her teeth while she decided whether to undress in the bathroom or the bedroom. Then she realized that her pyjamas were still under her pillow.

......

When Lucy returned to the bedroom, Jack grinned at her as he entered the bathroom in his turn. "Won't be long," he said.

She noticed that all he had done during her absence was to hang their anoraks in the wardrobe, remove his shoes and socks and turn back both sides of the bed.

"He's leaving the decision to me," she thought, feeling pleased at his consideration.

She undressed quickly and reached for her pyjamas. But she was not quite quick enough and only had the trousers on when the door behind her opened.

All Jack could see was Lucy's bare back as she leant over the bed.

"Sorry; I should've given you more warning," he called apologetically, "but I must say you've got a terrific back! I can even see the outline of your trapezius, not to mention the superb deltoids. No wonder you made short shift of that telephone directory!"

To cover the shock of his sudden appearance, Lucy laughed and said: "That reminds me: we never had our directory tearing competition. Anyway, I had no idea you were so knowledgeable about the muscles of the upper back; you didn't know much about legs in Terregles."

"Those two particular muscles are about the only ones I know," Jack admitted. "Some teenage boys at the club where I help were showing off one evening flexing their backs and arms. The trainer used one lad with remarkably good muscle definition as a demonstration model. But your back is far superior and you're not even bracing your shoulders!"

Then Lucy really surprised him. "I'll do that if you like, provided you come and massage me," she said softly, dropping her pyjama jacket on the bed and raising her arms in typical bodybuilder pose.

Jack eagerly moved over to lovingly caress her strong neck and shoulders before using the forefinger of each hand to follow the outline of her hard diamond-shaped trapezius. Starting at her neck, his fingers ran symmetrically down towards her shoulders. On meeting her powerful deltoids, they changed direction and swept down in two long arcs to meet almost halfway down her spine.

His hands then returned to begin kneading her rock-hard deltoids, but it was almost impossible to do the job properly. "Your back is incredible," he whispered, "but, if I'm to massage it properly, you'll need to lie face down on the bed and relax."

The next ten minutes were a delight to them both. Jack rejoiced at such intimate contact and Lucy found his hands not only doing a splendid job but also causing her to have feelings she had never known before.

"You're really good at massaging," she said. "Can we do it regularly? I'll return the favour of course."

"By all means," he replied, overjoyed at the thought and wondering what might happen next.

However, Lucy merely reached for her pyjama top and rather awkwardly slipped it on before turning to him with an uncharacteristically shy and apologetic smile.

"May we just get into bed and have a hug before we go to sleep. I'm not quite ready for anything further yet. I hope you don't mind too much," she said softly.

Jack remembered what he had determined to do – to put her first at all times.

"I love you so much that I'll be as patient as you like," he said, trying not to show his disappointment.

Chapter 15: Return to Carlisle

Lucy and Jack had just finished breakfast on their last morning when the waitress hurried over looking worried.

"There's a policeman in reception asking to see you," she whispered, anxious not to alarm the other people in the room.

The young couple quickly thanked her for looking after them for the short time they had been there and Jack slipped a banknote into her hand before they went to see what the man wanted.

He looked relieved when he saw them and, in somewhat broken English, informed them that the woman had been arrested late the previous evening and that he had been sent to ask them to come to the police station to identify her. Unfortunately, she had just had time to throw her handgun into the trees before the police reached her. As it had been getting too dark to undertake a proper search for the weapon, one had recommenced early that morning. There had been no sign of her two associates but a car believed to have been hired by them was being investigated and might yield further clues.

"I have a car outside and will take you as soon as you are ready," he concluded.

"We'll collect our luggage straight away because we have a bus to catch at 8:52 and don't want to risk missing our flight at Basle airport," Jack said.

"I've been instructed to drive you to Frutigen if necessary," the man assured them as they hurried upstairs.

......

At first, it seemed that the friendly policeman was driving them in the wrong direction until they remembered that, as pedestrians, they had been able to cross the River Allenbach on a footbridge, thus making the journey to the village centre much shorter.

It did not take long for them to confirm the identity of the woman who had twice been quite close to them. She was

111

sitting in the only cell of the small establishment with a defiant expression on her surly face and still wearing the easily recognisable but now very crumpled tweed suit that had looked so out of place in a warm sunny meadow high above Adelboden.

Lucy and Jack had barely returned to the outer office with their guide when the front door opened and two weary policemen entered. They were, however, looking extremely pleased with themselves: one was carrying a transparent plastic bag containing a handgun.

The officer on duty at the desk commended them in a burst of rapid German before turning to Jack and making an effort to speak more slowly.

Jack interpreted to Lucy. "He wants us to see if we can recognise it."

The young couple went through the motions but Jack soon had to confess that most small guns would look the same to them, especially if only seen from a few metres away.

Their friendly police driver returned just in time to overhear this last comment. "Never mind; it was found close to where we caught her and will almost certainly have her fingerprints on it," he said. "If you're ready, I'll take you to Frutigen."

......

Not much more than an hour later, Lucy and Jack were on the platform of Spiez station when IC61 swept in on its way from Interlaken to Basle.

"It's amazing to think that these express trains come through here every 30 minutes at busy times of the day," Lucy commented.

"No lack of passengers either," Jack replied, as they search for two adjacent seats.

"All good things come to an end," Lucy remarked sadly when they were seated at last. "I'm going to miss Switzerland and all our adventures."

They gazed nostalgically out over Lake Thun for the short time it took to reach the town of the same name.

......

It was not until the rapidly passing scenery became less interesting after leaving Berne that Lucy suddenly remembered the small New Testament in her shoulder bag.

"I must look up that verse from Romans, Chapter 10," she thought. "After all; because of it we were saved from almost certain discovery."

Jack was dozing by this time and did not notice what she was doing until there was a gentle nudge on his elbow. The small volume lay open on her lap and she had been slowly turning the pages.

"Look at this," she said. "I was trying to find the Bible verse we saw on the card and came across this passage in one of the Gospels." She tilted the small book so that they could read together.

"It's lucky I've got good eyesight," Jack muttered as he followed her moving finger.

"For God so loved the world that he gave his one and only Son, that whoever believes in him shall not perish but have eternal life. For God did not send his Son into the world to condemn the world, but to save the world through him. Whoever believes in him is not condemned..." (John, Ch.3, vv.16-18)

Jack sat back looking stunned and was silent for moment.

Then he spoke just loud enough for Lucy to hear: "If I'd seen those words a couple of days ago, I'd have thought nothing of them, but now, somehow, it's different!"

Lucy looked at him with understanding. "It's the same for me," she replied, "even though I think I heard them not long ago when I went to church with my foster parents – just to please them!"

Jack nodded. "In view of what happened yesterday, I can only conclude that there must be a God," he said thoughtfully.

113

"I just don't believe that, under normal circumstances, a person can look straight at you without seeing you or that a hand reaching for a gun can suddenly freeze. Perhaps we should investigate the claims of Christianity together, although I have no idea how to start."

"Yes, let's do that!" Lucy said with determination. "I'm sure my parents' advice would be to start by asking God to help us."

"Can you do it? I've no idea how to pray," Jack admitted.

Lucy was suddenly conscious that the railway carriage was crowded and anything they said could be overheard. Nevertheless, she somehow knew it was important to take this first step and so she leaned towards her companion and whispered close to his ear.

"Lord God, thank you for hearing our cry for help yesterday and answering so amazingly. Please guide us now as we seek to find out more about Jesus."

The young couple looked at each other, wondering what might unfold. At least they knew they were in this new adventure together.

......

Things began to happen sooner than expected. In the aircraft, Jack was stowing their backpacks in one of the overhead lockers while Lucy settled herself in the centre of a row of three seats when the middle-aged man in the window position turned to her with a pleasant smile. With considerable surprise she saw he was wearing a dog-collar and must be a Christian cleric of some sort.

When Jack took the outer seat, he noticed that Lucy was introducing herself to her neighbour. "That's odd, Lucy's not normally so friendly with strangers," he thought and was even more taken aback when she introduced him as well.

It was only after the routine demonstration of the safety equipment and the plane was slowly moving towards the runway that the conversation recommenced and the young couple explained that they had just spent a delightful week trail-running in the Alps. The friendly cleric, who gave his name as George, was clearly impressed.

"It's wonderful to be young," he murmured nostalgically before raising his voice again. "You clearly had a splendid time but have managed to retain the excitement of folk just about to start an adventure. People usually return home wishing their holiday could have lasted longer; I know I do!"

He looked at them enquiringly, not wanting to intrude but sure there was something God wanted him to say to this attractive couple.

Lucy smiled at him. "Well, we did become engaged last night, which is exciting enough, but something else happened as well."

She proceeded to explain what had occurred on the slopes above Adelboden, only pausing while the plane hurtled down the runway and became airborne.

Her account was an accurate but shortened version and concluded with the words in St John's Gospel that she had come across on the train journey.

George listened intently before remaining quiet for several seconds; so long in fact that the young couple began to wonder if he believed their story.

"I have absolutely no doubt that you've experienced something supernatural," he said eventually. "Almighty God has clearly been reaching out to you. For example, it was not by accident that someone left a scripture card on the café table and your friend used it to write down his 'phone number. As for the thug who failed to see you, I came across something similar years ago when I read about a Christian evangelist who had been smuggling illegal Bibles into a Communist country. They were in plain sight at the top of his suitcase but the customs official failed to see them when he opened the lid!"

"When you responded with that prayer on the train a few hours ago you were effectively giving God – who always respects our freewill – permission to reveal more of his plan for your lives. So again, it's no accident that we're sitting together and I'm ready to help in any way I can."

George stopped and looked at Lucy and Jack expectantly.

Lucy suddenly felt at a loss and was relieved when Jack unexpectedly took over.

"Lucy used to go to church sometimes with her foster parents but I'm almost totally ignorant, so please tell us in a nutshell what the Christian faith is all about?" he said.

George took a deep breath. "In essence, it's all about Jesus," he said slowly, echoing Jack's phrase, "and the need to meet him as a person and respond to what he accomplished for us on the Cross.

"All human beings, however good they may appear to be, fall short of the perfection of a holy God. In Matthew 5:48, it's recorded that Jesus told his listeners: "Be perfect as your heavenly Father is perfect". He wouldn't have said this if there was no hope of it ever happening. But the problem is that we're sinners and very far from God's perfection. We therefore deserve to be subject to his judgement against sin. God, however, also embodies perfect love and does not want to have to condemn the objects of his love.

"The only solution in this humanly impossible situation was for God to take the initiative and pay the penalty himself. I find a helpful analogy in the picture of a judge passing sentence on an offender and then coming down from the bench and paying the fine that he himself imposed.

"In reality, this happened when Jesus, the sinless Son of God, was born into this fallen world, lived, taught and healed as no man has ever done, and then willingly died an undeserved death on the Cross. He endured not only the physical agony of that barbaric form of Roman execution, but, even worse, God's judgement against the totality of human sin. For those terrible hours on the Cross, Jesus experienced the utter dereliction of taking responsibility for the failure of all human beings. The proof that he succeeded is evidenced by the fact that he rose from the dead – the day we celebrate on Easter Sunday – and appeared to the disciples and many other people. But God's forgiveness is not automatic; there has to be some measure of belief and response on our part.

"All I've said will only make sense when God himself reveals Jesus to you. This is, I believe, what he has already begun, as evidenced by the miraculous happenings in Adelboden. Eventually, it will be up to you to believe or not. The step that we all need to take is to acknowledge that we need a Saviour, thank him and accept what he has done for us. I did when I was 17 years old and have never regretted my decision."

George sat back in his seat with relief, conscious that his explanation might have been overcomplicated. Lucy seemed to have been absorbing his words like a sponge but Jack was clearly finding it harder and sat with a puzzled frown on his expressive face.

Lucy took his hand and squeezed it tight, not in the vice-like grip she had used on their first encounter but with the grip of a lover who would stick with her beloved through thick and thin. Jack had been there for her during her times of difficulty, now she would stand with him.

"We'll see this through together," she whispered.

George closed his eyes and appeared to be dozing, but, in the heavenly realm, his prayers for the young couple beside him were rising like incense and, completely unknown to them, barriers were crumbling.

......

The sound system suddenly sprang to life; "This is your Captain speaking. I hope you have had a comfortable journey. We are now about to begin our descent into London Heathrow...."

The fasten-seatbelts signs lit up and the whole cabin stirred to life.

"May I pray for you before we land?" George asked as the three of them belted up.

"Yes please," Lucy replied and Jack nodded appreciatively.

There followed a very short prayer that left the young couple almost stunned. George appeared to be speaking to a much loved friend as he committed his companions into the care of a loving God who would never let them down.

Lucy thanked him quietly and George handed her a card bearing his name and contact details: it transpired that he was based at a church in Doncaster. "If I can be of any help in the future, just give me a call or send me an email," he said.

......

Lucy and Jack parted company with the friendly cleric soon after passing through passport control because he had to wait for his suitcase to emerge on a conveyor belt. Their parting handshakes were so warm that Jack wondered if they should give him their contact details, but Lucy sensed that George wanted to leave them totally free to be the ones initiating further contact should they feel the need to do so.

The young couple therefore hurried on with their backpacks and eventually found their way to the Heathrow Express station in the basement of Terminal 5 where trains left for Paddington every 15 minutes. Once there, they would have to join the Circle Line to reach Euston for a fast train to Carlisle.

......

Lucy was thankful that the bedroom John had booked for them in the Hotel Ibis close to Carlisle station was fairly quiet, although she was slightly disconcerted to find that it only had a double bed, albeit a large one.

Jack noticed immediately. "Don't worry; I think we're both far too tired to do anything except have a nice hot shower and good long sleep. I know I'm even more exhausted than after our arduous run over to Kandersteg and back!"

118

Lucy grinned. "Not to mention hungry; apart from a good breakfast back in Adelboden, we've existed on snacks," she said as she headed for the bathroom.

"Thank goodness we had a boiled egg this morning," Jack replied. "The breakfast here is not included in the room price and so I'll get you a real English breakfast in a nice café tomorrow before we go to John's office."

But he was speaking into thin air: Lucy had already begun to run her shower.

Chapter 16: Denouement

Jack had a dream that night; at least he assumed it was a dream when he recalled it later. He dreamt that their hotel bedroom was filled with light. His immediate thought was that Lucy must have gone to the bathroom and left the door open with the light on. But then he realised that this light had a quality never encountered before; it did not appear to be emanating from inside the room, and, even stranger, took the form of shimmering waves that slowly descended to cover both him and the sleeping girl beside him. As each wave intensified in its turn, he was conscious of being bathed in a love so all-embracing as to be beyond comprehension. He had never felt more alive.

Just as Jack was wondering if he should wake Lucy so that she could share the experience, a gentle voice spoke: "Know this Jack; even if you and Lucy were the only people on earth who needed a Saviour, I would have died for you."

There was complete silence for a moment and the light began to fade. Before complete darkness returned, however, and almost as if to bring Jack back to reality, the quiet voice added, with a hint of humour: "Be sure to tell Lucy what you have seen and heard before taking her to that breakfast you promised her."

The next thing Jack knew was awaking from a deep sleep with the sound of his small alarm clock buzzing in his ear; it was precisely 8:30. Lucy was already in the bathroom and the small kettle on the dressing table had just boiled ready for their cups of coffee.

......

It was only when they were fully dressed that Jack sat beside Lucy on the bed and told her what had transpired in the middle of the night. He half expected her to express disappointment at missing the experience, but she responded with one of the special smiles reserved only for him.

"So now you believe as well," she said softly. "What are we going to do about it?"

"I'm ready to pray the way George suggested but I don't have the words," the reply came. "Can you do it for both of us?"

"Most willingly," she said, "although I don't think the precise words matter if we pray from the bottom of our hearts."

She took his hand before continuing. "Lord Jesus, we are still very ignorant but thank you for arranging for us to meet George. We certainly don't deserve the amazing love that took you to the Cross but we really believe that you died so that our sinfulness could be forgiven and we might receive a life that extends beyond death. Please take us and lead us in the way you want us to go. Amen."

"Amen," Jack echoed for the first meaningful time in his life.

The young couple looked at each other for a moment or two. "I don't know about you but something indefinable has changed deep inside me," Jack said slowly.

"Yes, it's the same for me," Lucy whispered.

They hugged lovingly before getting their things together ready for departure and the long anticipated breakfast.

By ten o'clock they were sitting in a pleasant café in the centre of the town. A full English breakfast and proper pot of tea had never tasted so good.

......

John greeted Lucy and Jack like returning heroes when they reached his office at eleven o'clock.

"You two have succeeded brilliantly," he said. "Our Swiss friend was so delighted to have the 1721 manuscript back that he's not only paid my company a bonus in addition to our fee but says that he wants to reward you in some way and will be in touch with me again later. The trusted servant who collected the package must have taken a discrete photo of you in the Kandersteg restaurant because I've also been

121

congratulated on my choice of couriers! Now tell me all about it."

The young couple launched into a brief summary of their time in the Alps, concluding with the attempt by the Russian mafia to waylay them. Jack also informed John that Lucy and he had become engaged.

"I'm so glad; my congratulations!" John exclaimed. "That gives me another excuse to take you out to lunch before you catch your train home. Other reasons are, of course, a job well done, and, what you don't yet know, the arrest the Bodleian mole. He was actually caught red-handed in the process of composing an email and trying to send it. You'll never guess what it said."

Jack and Lucy shook their heads, completely at a loss, and John supplied his punch line. "It went something like: "The manuscript will be delivered to Kandersteg by the couple in the attached picture. The address is......" That's when the wretched man was interrupted, although unfortunately he managed to press the send button before he could be stopped. Your picture had been copied somehow from the security camera at the Library reception desk."

Lucy looked at Jack. "Jack surmised as much on that last exciting day in Adelboden," she reported with a hint of pride. "Over lunch we'll tell you how we escaped the mafia thugs, although you may have difficulty believing us!"

Chapter 17: Epilogue

It was a fine summer day in mid-August and sunlight bathed the valley below the restaurant terrace where Lucy and Jack were enjoying a cup of coffee. They had married five days earlier in the church in Lancaster attended by Lucy's foster parents; in fact, her foster father had been the one to give her away.

Apart from arranging the wedding, a lot of other things had happened during the nine weeks since the young couple's engagement back in early June. Jack had given up his flat in Leeds and come to share Lucy's small flat on the outskirts of Lancaster and would be taking up a research fellowship at Lancaster University in September. Lucy, meanwhile, had found a satisfying and enjoyable job as a fitness trainer in a health club, working under the direction of a physiotherapist specializing in the rehabilitation of people recovering from physical injury. They had also found a church where they had received a warm welcome and been baptized.

Everything had happened so quickly that the young couple were still finding it hard to take in the fact that they really were married. The location of their honeymoon was even more surprising; was the village nestling in the valley below them really Grindelwald? And was that beautiful mountain rising in solitary splendour a few miles away really the Wetterhorn? Or was it all just a wonderful dream?

......

In fact, they were in the Alps again and it had all come about thanks to the extraordinary generosity of the retired Swiss businessman.

At their debriefing meeting in Carlisle, John had told them of the wealthy man's delight at the return of Peter the Great's manuscript, once so prized by his parents, and of his intention to reward the young couriers in some way. His determination had increased even further when he had learned of their close encounter with the Russian mafia and even more on being told about their engagement.

Lucy and Jack had been dumbfounded when they discovered the extent of the reward; their benefactor had sent them, via John's company, business-class Swiss Air tickets from London to Zurich, to be used at their convenience anytime within the following six months, and a Visa card allowing them access to 4,000 CHF to spend on accommodation and other expenditure in Switzerland.

The young couple had merely had to fund their travel in the UK, a single night's accommodation, and, in view of the high cost of travel in Switzerland, a half-price railcard purchased from the SSB website. Jack had also wisely suggested making the 4,000 CHF last 12 nights by arranging for them to stay three nights at Lara and Daniel Geber's guesthouse in Wilderswil – thus allowing Lucy to satisfy her desire to take some trips on a lake steamer – and the remaining time in a modest hotel in Wengen on half-board basis.

They had chosen the venerable chalet-style Hotel Edelweiss and made the on-line booking because they had been attracted by its picture on the website and quiet but convenient location near the village centre. It was only halfway through their stay that they discovered the hotel manager and his wife were Christians.

......

Swiss Air operates out of Terminal 2 at Heathrow and Lucy had been most surprised when Jack ushered her into one of the first-class lounges open to Swiss Air business-class passengers.

"This really is luxury!" she exclaimed when she saw the refreshments available. They tucked in, having had no breakfast at the so-called budget hotel near the airport. She was also surprised when a light meal was served during the flight.

"I'm sorry I won't be able to offer you this treatment when we fly at our own expense," Jack whispered.

Lucy smiled. "It's just nice to have the one-off experience," she responded.

Once in Switzerland, they had had to change trains in Berne and wait a short time for the familiar intercity IC61 to Interlaken. The journey time was almost the same as it had been from Basle, however, because Zurich airport has its own rail station with fast trains to Berne and no bus transfer is required.

......

Now, on their fifth day in Switzerland, Lucy and Jack had spent one night in the Hotel Edelweiss in a comfortable bedroom with a good shower. The excellent four-course dinner turned out to be a set meal with no choice; clearly one of the ways of achieving prices that were surprisingly reasonable by Swiss standards.

After a wonderful night, excellent breakfast and a time of prayer back in their bedroom, they had just completed the first leg of the day's trail run, leaving Wengen to climb gradually up over Kleine Scheidegg and down as far as the Brandegg restaurant overlooking Grindelwald. It was busier than it had been in early June and the sun warmer, but, in a way, they felt they had returned close to where their adventure had started.

"This is bliss!" Lucy said as she soaked up the sun.

But she was never still for long. "Time to head back over the mountains to Wengen," she declared. "But tomorrow, weather permitting, I'd love to go further. What about coming this way again, going right down into Grindelwald and then seeing how far we can get towards the Wetterhorn; it looks so attractive. If necessary, we could always just come back as far as Grindelwald and get the train to Wengen via Lauterbrunnen."

Jack nodded happily in agreement. "What a girl! She continues to delight and astonish me," he mused.

......

125

After another excellent evening meal, followed by self-service coffee in the small resident's lounge-cum-library, they returned to their bedroom, tired but happy after the energetic day. Lucy sat on the bed and gestured for Jack to take the easy chair. She glanced at the small wall-mounted TV set wondering whether to try it out but then decided against it.

Jack looked at his companion's delightful profile. "I think I'm more in love with her every day," he thought and was just about to say so out loud when she turned back towards him. It was no longer necessary; their eyes conveyed far more than mere words.

Slowly, she rose to her feet and began to undress; the message was obvious and he gently helped her remove the gentian-blue dress that he had bought her as a wedding gift and carefully hung it up in the wardrobe, together with his shirt.

When he turned back, she was standing looking at him shyly, so completely different from the proud girl first encountered in the officers' mess at the army base near Carlisle.

"You're astonishingly beautiful: perfect in every way," he breathed in complete awe.

"Thank you for the compliment, but my bust is too small to warrant that description," she said rather sadly.

"No! Your figure is just right; ideal for such a superb athlete!"

She looked at him with a smile that lit up her lovely eyes.

This was the prelude to the next wonderful hour.

Afterwards, Jack had the almost inexpressible joy of holding his sleeping wife in his arms until he too fell fast asleep.

L - #0075 - 240119 - C0 - 210/148/7 - PB - DID2422475